"Daddy sold himself to Nicholas Bristow!"

Alison took hold of her mother's hand. "Are you seriously suggesting I should do the same thing?"

Mrs. Mortimer thumped the coverlet with her fist. "For heaven's sake, you're being offered the chance to recover everything we've lost, together with the kind of husband most girls would fight over."

"Maybe I'd prefer a man who wasn't quite so universally attractive," Alison said dryly.

Mrs. Mortimer threw herself back on her pillows, looking agitated. "Dear, it isn't given to us all to fall deeply in love. Very satisfactory relationships have been known to evolve from very little."

After a time, Alison pushed her hair back from her face and dropped a light kiss on her mother's cheek. "Don't look so worried. Uncle Hugh said Daddy was a gambler.... I must be more like him than I thought."

SARA CRAVEN probably had the ideal upbringing for a budding writer. She grew up by the seaside in a house crammed with books, with a box of old clothes to dress up in and a swing outside in a walled garden. She produced the opening of her first book at age five and is eternally grateful to her mother for having kept a straight face. Now she has more than twenty-five romance novels to her credit. The author is married with two children.

Books by Sara Craven

HARLEQUIN PRESENTS
459—WITCHING HOUR
487—DARK SUMMER DAWN
551—UNGUARDED MOMENT
561—COUNTERFEIT BRIDE
599—SUP WITH THE DEVIL
616—PAGAN ADVERSARY
647—A BAD ENEMY
704—DARK PARADISE
815—ALIEN VENGEANCE
832—ACT OF BETRAYAL
856—PROMISE OF THE UNICORN
872—ESCAPE ME NEVER

HARLEQUIN ROMANCE
1943—THE GARDEN OF DREAMS

These books may be available at your local bookseller.

Don't miss any of our special offers. Write to us at the following address for information on our newest releases.

Harlequin Reader Service
901 Fuhrmann Blvd., P.O. Box 1397, Buffalo, NY 14240
Canadian address: P.O. Box 603,
Fort Erie, Ont. L2A 9Z9

SARA CRAVEN

a high price to pay

Harlequin Books

TORONTO • NEW YORK • LONDON
AMSTERDAM • PARIS • SYDNEY • HAMBURG
STOCKHOLM • ATHENS • TOKYO • MILAN

Harlequin Presents first edition October 1986
ISBN 0-373-10920-2

Original hardcover edition published in 1986
by Mills & Boon Limited

CHAPTER ONE

'THAT man—what's he doing here?'

Alison Mortimer hoped devoutly that her mother's angry whisper to her had been sufficiently drowned by the organ music to prevent it reaching the ears of the other mourners in the small church.

And particularly, she thought with embarrassment, the ears of the man in question, who was stationed only a few pews away.

She'd been conscious of him, of course, from the moment they'd arrived. Nicholas Bristow was a distinctive figure, not easily overlooked, and Alison had noticed his tall, black-haired figure with a twinge of alarm that she'd resolutely told herself was really surprise.

The notice in the paper had said firmly that the funeral service was to be private, and she hadn't thought Nicholas Bristow a sufficiently close friend of her late father to ignore such a pointed hint.

She saw gratefully that Uncle Hugh had taken her mother's hand and given it a comforting pat, while murmuring something soothing, and registering at the same time the uneasy look he exchanged with Aunt Beth.

She moved her shoulders restively. There it was again—that feeling, growing almost to conviction, that there was something going on—something wrong, over and above the appalling reality of her father's sudden collapse and death, only a few days before.

If she hadn't been so frantically busy, trying to run the house as usual, make the arrangements for the funeral, calm her mother, who was almost hysterical with shock, grief and rage at her loss, and comfort her younger sister Melanie, summoned home from boarding school for the funeral, she would have found out what was happening—pinned Uncle Hugh down, and made him tell her why he found it so apparently difficult to meet her gaze any more, she thought grimly.

But once the ordeal of the funeral was behind her, and the obligation of the buffet lunch waiting for them back at Ladymead had been fulfilled, she could start finding out.

She could also, she thought, a lump rising in her throat, get a chance to mourn for her father herself.

She glanced at her mother, ethereal in black, her thin hands nervously pulling at her handkerchief, and sighed. Catherine Mortimer had never been a strong woman, physically or emotionally. All her married life she had depended totally on her husband, and more latterly on her elder daughter as well. How she would cope with the everyday realities of widowhood, once the drama of the funeral and, later, the memorial service, was over, Alison hadn't the faintest idea.

Mrs Mortimer had enjoyed her position as the wife of the area's leading industrialist. She had loved being asked to take the chair at local organisations, presiding at dinner parties, and playing the hostess for housefuls of weekend guests, although the donkey work of these occasions had always been left to Alison.

Things would be very different from now on,

she thought, although there would be no shortage of money. Anthony Mortimer had left his family well provided for from his shareholdings in the light engineering works which his grandfather had pioneered.

Her mother might have to step down from being the locality's First Lady, but she would be able to maintain her comfortable existence, adding to her porcelain collection, and playing bridge with her cronies. She might even take a greater interest in the day-to-day running of Ladymead, Alison told herself without a great deal of conviction.

She knew perfectly well that the mundane details of housekeeping had never appealed to her mother. She had relied completely on the elderly and supremely efficient housekeeper, Mrs Wharton, who had been installed at Ladymead since her husband's boyhood. And after Mrs Wharton's death, the chores of making sure everything ran like clockwork, of engaging staff, and paying the bills had been handed over, charmingly but definitely, to Alison.

'Such good practice for you, darling, when it comes to running a home of your own,' Mrs Mortimer had said sweetly.

But Alison hadn't been fooled for a minute. Her mother had been a dazzlingly pretty woman when she was younger, and Melanie was blossoming into real beauty with every month that passed, but Alison herself had been born, and remained, an ugly duckling. She was small and slight with light brown hair, clear hazel eyes, and a pale skin which had a distressing tendency to flush when she was disturbed or embarrassed, and as she was a shy girl, this happened far more often than she wished.

She had no idea why this should be so. Both her

mother and Mel were miracles of self-possession, and her father had been a cheerfully ebullient man too.

'You must be a changeling, darling,' her mother had sometimes teased her.

And sometimes she felt like it, Alison acknowledged ruefully.

Perhaps if her school exam results had been dazzling like Mel's promised to be, rather than respectable, she might have broken out of the mould she could see being prepared for her, and insisted on university and a career of some kind. But with no very firm idea of what she would like to do with her life, it had been difficult for her to resist the pressure from her family to stay at home and run Ladymead for her mother. But she had been determined to achieve at least a measure of independence for herself, and had managed to find herself a part-time job in a local estate agent's office. She had been hired in the first instance under the vague heading of Girl Friday, which Alison had silently translated as 'dogsbody', but she had amazed herself, and her new employer, by discovering an unexpected talent for actually selling houses. In spite of her shyness, she had the knack of matching properties to potential buyers, many of whom preferred her quiet efficiency to the 'hard sell' they were often subjected to. Simon Thwaite, her boss, had concealed his astonishment, given her a rise, and asked if she would be prepared to work full time, an offer she had regretfully had to refuse. He had also asked her out to dinner, which she had accepted, and they had enjoyed several pleasant evenings in each other's company.

But that, she knew, was as far as it went. She

couldn't see herself having a serious relationship with Simon, or any of the other men she came across, and had come to the conclusion that she was probably one of nature's spinsters.

And probably just as well, she thought without self-pity, because the evidence suggested that from now on her mother was going to need her more than ever.

Driving back to Ladymead after the service, Mrs Mortimer was volubly tearful.

'So much to endure still,' she said, clinging to her brother's arm. 'Dear Hugh—such a tower of strength! And now this dreadful lunch to get through somehow.' Her brows snapped together. 'I hope that Bristow man hasn't had the gall to invite himself to that! If so, you must deal with it, Hugh. He must be made to see this is a very personal, family occasion, and that, as a stranger, he is intruding on our grief.'

Hugh Bosworth cleared his throat uncomfortably. 'It might be better not to say or do anything hasty,' he said heavily. 'After all, Anthony did a lot of business with the fellow.'

'Did he?' Mrs Mortimer dabbed at her eyes with her handkerchief. 'He never discussed business matters with me, of course. I've never had a head for that sort of thing.' A fresh sense of grievance struck her. 'And I don't understand why Mr Liddell is insisting on going over poor Anthony's will with me. I know what's in it—he explained it all most carefully to me, and to Alison when he drew it up. There'll be duties, of course, but apart from that, he made it all as simple as possible.' She began to cry again. 'Although I never thought ... I was always sure I'd be the first ...'

Hugh Bosworth patted her shoulder, looking,

his niece thought judiciously, positively hunted.
Again she felt that faint *frisson* of unease. She
wished she could have spoken to Aunt Beth, but
Mrs Bosworth was following in the next car with
Melanie.

Back at the house, Alison swiftly checked that
arrangements for the lunch had been carried out as
impeccably as usual, then went upstairs to take off
the jacket of her simple dark grey suit, and tidy
her hair. As she dragged a comb through her neat
shoulder-length bob, she heard the first of the cars
arrive to disgorge its passengers at the front door.
Mentally, she reviewed who should be arriving. As
well as Anthony Mortimer's closest friends, there
would be a few of his co-directors from the works.

She gave a faint sigh. They would be worried.
Anthony Mortimer had been the linchpin of the
company, believing in it, backing it to the hilt
always. She wasn't sure how they would replace him.

She gave a last look at herself in the mirror,
and grimaced. She could win a nondescript prize,
she thought candidly as she turned away. And saw
from the window Nicholas Bristow alighting from
the last car and standing on the drive, staring at
the house.

Alison groaned inwardly. Her mother had
overreacted to his presence at the church, of
course, but there was a certain amount of
justification for her attitude. He was a stranger to
them, no matter how close he might or might not
have been to her father. He had been to Ladymead
only once before, for dinner, and had annoyed
Mrs Mortimer by spending the latter part of the
evening closeted in the study with her husband.

'So inconsiderate!' Mrs Mortimer had com-
plained fretfully to Alison. 'A dinner party should

be a social occasion, and your father knows how I
feel about business being mixed with pleasure.'

Alison had thought wryly that probably her
father's wishes has not had a great deal to do with
it. She had had Nicholas Bristow as her dinner
partner, and had found him arrogantly intim-
idating.

He was the kind of man, she was forced to
admit, that most women would find very
attractive. Coupled with that unmistakable aura of
wealth and power which fitted him as well as his
elegant clothes, he possessed an individual brand
of compelling, almost insolent good looks. He
probably had charm too, only Alison hadn't been
privileged to encounter it. Eyes as blue and chill as
a winter's sky had travelled over her, remembered
with difficulty that she had been introduced to him
on arrival as the daughter of the house, and made
it clear he found her wanting in every respect.

He had responded to her conversational over-
tures civilly, but without enthusiasm, and it was
obvious that his thoughts were elsewhere most of
the time.

If it hadn't been so hurtful, it would almost have
been amusing, Alison decided, hating him cor-
dially.

She had no time for that kind of sexy male
arrogance, and she couldn't understand what he
could possibly have in common with her genial,
outgoing father.

For starters, Nicholas Bristow was at least
twenty-five years her father's junior. One of the
City's boy wonders, she could remember reading
about him somewhere. A whizz-kid financier with
the Midas touch. In his thirties now, of course, but
still apparently printing his own money.

It was—heartening to believe that he had thought highly enough of her father to come to his funeral, even without an invitation. Only Alison didn't believe it. According to the items about him in the various gossip columns which appeared with such monotonous regularity, Nicholas Bristow didn't give a damn about anything except making money. He wasn't married, but he certainly wasn't celibate either, seeming to change the ladies in his life as frequently as his expensive suits.

She might have contempt for his lifestyle, but at the same time Alison had him mentally filed as someone it could be dangerous to offend, and she decided it could be wise to intervene before he came face to face with her mother.

He was in the hall, as Alison came downstairs, in the act of handing his coat to Mrs Horner, the daily help.

Alison said with a coolness she was far from feeling, 'It's all right, Mrs Horner. I'll deal with this.'

At the sound of her voice Nicholas Bristow turned, his brows rising interrogatively as he looked at her. Once again the sheer force of his attraction struck her like a body blow. How fortunate that his personality didn't match, Alison thought stonily as she walked down the last remaining stairs.

She said, 'Good morning, Mr Bristow. I don't suppose you remember me.'

'Indeed I do, Miss Mortimer.'

She prayed she wouldn't blush like a schoolgirl and ruin everything. Aloud, she said quietly, 'This is rather embarrassing for us, Mr Bristow, but it seems there's been a slight misunderstanding. It was kind of you to come to my father's funeral service, but this lunch is restricted to family and close friends, and unfortunately . . .'

'Unfortunately, I don't fall within either category,' Nicholas Bristow supplied calmly. 'I'm aware of that, Miss Mortimer.'

'Then I'm sure you won't wish to intrude,' Alison said, lifting her chin a little. 'My mother, as you can imagine, is in a very nervous and distressed condition, and can't be expected to cope with uninvited guests.'

'Yes, I can well imagine.' His firm mouth twisted slightly. 'But the misunderstanding is yours, Miss Mortimer. As it happens, I have been invited here. By Alec Liddell, and also by your uncle, Colonel Bosworth.'

Alison's lips parted helplessly in a little gasp. 'They—did? But why?'

'I suggest you ask them,' he drawled. 'And while you're conducting your little interrogation, I'll wait quietly somewhere where the sight of me won't cause your mother any problems.' As she hesitated he added quietly, 'I'm no gatecrasher, Miss Mortimer. I do have a reason to be here.'

She said levelly, 'I don't pretend to understand what's going on, but perhaps you'd wait in the study while I speak to my uncle.' She led the way across the hall and opened the door. It was quite a small room, panelled in oak, the heavy curtains still drawn out of respect. It was the first time Alison had entered the room since her father's death, and it seemed at once still so redolent of his personality that she checked abruptly in the doorway, her whole body tautening.

She was hardly aware of the sharp look from the man beside her, but she heard him say, 'I think the situation would be improved by some daylight, don't you?' followed by the rattle of the rings along the poles as he drew back the curtains, allowing some watery spring sunshine to permeate the room.

She was back in control again. 'Thank you,' she said huskily. 'There—there's some whisky in the corner cupboard, if you'd like to help yourself.'

'You're very hospitable.' The dry note in his voice wasn't lost on her. He walked across the room, and looked down at her, frowning slightly. 'I'm sorry about your father,' he said at last. 'I liked him.'

'Thank you.' Her voice was firmer this time. 'Now, you'll have to excuse me. I have to see to our—other guests.'

She closed the study door behind her quietly, and stood for a moment, forcing herself to think rapidly. It was an awful day, but it seemed to be getting worse with every moment that passed. She was more than uneasy now; she was getting frightened. From the chaos of the past week, some kind of monstrous pattern seemed to be emerging. She didn't understand it, nor did she want to. She wanted to run away somewhere and hide.

The atmosphere in the drawing room was inevitably subdued, but as Alison moved from group to group, thanking people for coming, and accepting their condolences, it occurred to her that everyone seemed abnormally gloomy and abstracted. Or was she being stupidly over-sensitive? she asked herself, making her way towards her uncle.

But before she could reach him, she was grabbed by Melanie.

'Who's the dish?' she hissed. 'And where have you hidden him?'

'I can't think who ...' Alison began, but Mel

gave her a little shake.

'Oh, don't be pompous, Ally! Tall and dark, with eyes like Paul Newman's. I saw him arrive.'

'You would,' Alison sighed. 'Well, his name's Nicholas Bristow, and he seems to be here on business.'

Melanie rolled her eyes in mock-lasciviousness. 'Do you think he'd do a deal with me?' She caught Alison's eye, and subsided. 'I'm sorry, Ally,' she muttered reluctantly. 'I know I shouldn't be making jokes at a time like this, but everything's so—so bloody!'

Alison put her arm round her sister's shoulders and gave her a swift hug. 'Yes, it is,' she said fiercely. 'And you make all the jokes you want. Now, I've got to talk to Uncle Hugh.'

'Hullo, my dear.' His voice was awkward. 'May I get you a drink?'

She shook her head. 'I'm not thirsty. I just want to know what's going on. Nicholas Bristow tells me you invited him here.'

'Well, it was Liddell's idea really.' He didn't meet her gaze. 'He felt it might make things—easier.'

'What things?' Alison's eyes narrowed. 'Uncle Hugh, you can't keep dropping hints like this. You've got to tell me!'

There was a silence, then he sighed heavily. 'Perhaps you have the right. I just don't know any more. And together, we might be able to cushion your mother . . .' He paused again. 'Did your father ever talk to you about money?'

She shook her head. 'I used to ask him, from time to time, especially about the works—if the company was being affected by the recession, but he always said everything was fine.'

He pulled her into a corner. 'Well, it wasn't fine,' he muttered. 'In fact, Ally, it was just about as bad as it could be. For the last two years he was pouring every penny he could raise into the firm, but it was never enough. Oh, he could have cut back, I suppose, but it would have meant laying men off, and he wouldn't do that. Said it was a bad sign, and reduced public confidence. Said he felt—responsible.'

Alison nodded. 'He did. Mortimers has always been a family company. Daddy hated the idea of redundancies. He felt it was a betrayal of people who trusted him.' She smiled sadly. 'A rather patriarchal attitude, I'm afraid.'

'A rather naïve one in this economic climate,' her uncle said grimly. 'And there was this house, of course, and your mother's—expenses.'

Alison hands clenched into fists at her side and she looked at him levelly. 'Uncle Hugh, are you trying to tell me that Daddy was broke?'

Unwillingly, he nodded. 'There's your mother's annuity, of course, that's safe. But as for the rest of it . . .'

'Oh, God!' Alison felt dazed, but she made herself think. 'But there are his shares in Mortimers, they must be worth something.'

'Only if the company itself has any value,' Colonel Bosworth said gloomily. 'And there's every chance of a receiver being put in.'

She bit her lip. 'Well—there's this house. I know it's big, and inconvenient, but Daddy had it valued not long ago, and if we sold it, and found somewhere smaller . . .'

He was shaking his head. 'That's what I'm trying to tell you, my dear.' His voice was awkward with compassion. 'The house, I'm afraid, he used as security for a considerable loan. Mortimers needed new machinery for a potential order from China—engineering components, I understand. It could have been the salvation of the place, and Anthony gambled everything on getting it.' He looked very old suddenly. 'Only he didn't. He got the news just before—just before . . .'

'His attack,' Alison said. She felt very cold, her body trembling uncontrollably. 'I—see. So—Ladymead doesn't belong to us any more. I—I can't quite believe it.' She closed her eyes for a moment. 'Poor Mummy? Where can she go? What can she do?'

'That is something we all have to discuss. But there need be no hasty decisions. I'm sure she'll be treated with every consideration by the—er—new owner.'

'New owner?' Her bewildered eyes searched his face. 'But you said the house had been used as security. It belongs to a bank, doesn't it?'

'Not as such.' Uncle Hugh looked more uncomfortable than ever. 'Your father had trouble in raising the money he wanted. It was felt, I think, that his proposition wasn't a good risk—as indeed it proved. The eventual loan was a—private arrangement, although perfectly legal, of course,' he added hastily.

Alison's nails scored the palms of her hands. She said unsteadily, 'It's—Nicholas Bristow, isn't it?'

Uncle Hugh nodded wretchedly, 'Yes.'

She whispered, 'Oh, God. So that's why . . .'

She couldn't say any more. She turned away, fighting her emotions, struggling to retain some rags of self-control as the full force of everything that had happened broke on her.

Crazily, a line from Shakespeare kept echoing and re-echoing in her head: 'One woe doth tread upon another's heels, so fast they follow.' And the upshot was that Ophelia was drowned, and she was drowning too, in anger and outrage and bewilderment.

At last she said brokenly, 'How could Daddy? How could he—mortgage our home to a stranger?'

'Because he was a gambler,' her uncle returned sombrely. 'Oh, not with cards or horses—that might have been easier to deal with. But he liked to take risks in business—unnecessary risks, like investing in these new machines without any guarantees from the Chinese that they'd ever be needed. I don't think the possibility of losing his gamble ever occurred to him. And give him his due, if Mortimers had won that contract, it would have been just the boost the works needed. He'd have been able to pay off the loan too, and neither your mother nor you and Melanie would ever have been any the wiser.'

'Only it didn't work out like that,' said Alison with a small mirthless smile. 'The problem now is—how do we break the news to Mother? How do we tell her she's not only penniless, but homeless too? And at the hands of a man she doesn't like. Or has Mr Bristow come to serve his notice to quit in person?'

'On the contrary.' Uncle Hugh looked almost affronted. 'You're doing him an injustice, Ally. He is most concerned.'

'How kind of him!' She pushed her hair back from her face with a shaking hand. 'But it doesn't change anything. He's not going to give us back our home, is he?'

'You have to be realistic, my dear.' Her uncle

looked horrified. 'No one could be expected simply to write off a debt of that magnitude. No, I'm afraid your poor father knew what he was risking when he entered into the arrangement—much against Alec Liddell's advice, I may say.'

'Bravo, Mr Liddell,' Alison said wearily. 'He'll be here soon, I suppose.'

'In about half an hour.' He nodded in affirmation. 'The others should be leaving by then. I thought we could all have a quiet chat—a family conclave, to decide what's best to be done.'

'And do you now count Nicholas Bristow as part of the family?'

There was an edge to her voice, and her uncle frowned rather reprovingly as he answered, 'No, of course not, child. But I'm sure it would be better for all concerned if matters were conducted on as—amicable a basis as possible. I know he's anxious to reassure your mother that he has no immediate plans to take possession.'

She winced. 'Don't!'

He shook his head. 'I'm sorry, Ally, but it's something you're going to have to come to terms with. Ladymead belongs to Nicholas Bristow now.'

She said softly, fiercely, 'Over my dead body.'

As she got to the study door, she heard Melanie's voice, and groaned inwardly. She turned the handle and went in. Melanie, flushed and bright-eyed, was draped decoratively across the arm of one of the big chairs, clearly in the middle of some anecdote which Nicholas Bristow was receiving with amused appreciation.

Alison said clearly and precisely, 'Would you go up to your room, Melanie, please. I have something I wish to say to Mr Bristow.'

For once Melanie didn't stop to argue. She took

one look at Alison's stormy eyes, at the bright spots of colour burning in the pallor of her face, and went without a word.

Alison closed the door behind her, then drew a deep breath before turning back to face him.

He said softly, 'Don't be angry with her, Miss Mortimer. You can't expect a kid of her age to join in day after day of undiluted gloom.'

He was seated on the edge of the big desk, glass in hand, swinging one elegantly shod foot. He had even, she noticed, loosened his tie slightly, and it was that detail which set the seal on her rage and bitterness.

'Get off my father's desk,' she said, her voice quivering. 'Get away from his things. They don't belong to you yet.'

He finished what was left in his glass and put it down, then got to his feet without haste.

'So he told you,' he observed expressionlessly.

'Yes, he told me.' She threw back her head defiantly, staring at him with disgust. 'I thought you were a financier, Mr Bristow, not a cheap money-lender!'

'Oh, I'm certainly not cheap, Miss Mortimer,' he said. He was smiling derisively, but there was anger simmering underneath, and she knew it. 'But do go on. I'm sure you can think of something appropriate about me preying on widows and orphans, if you really put your mind to it. Come on, sweetheart, let it rip. Don't leave a cliché unturned.'

'You bastard,' Alison said unevenly.

He clicked his tongue reprovingly. 'Not very inventive, or even true. Try again.'

She wrapped her arms round her body, shivering. 'You're vile,' she said quietly, after a pause. 'You've robbed us of everything, and you can stand there—taunting me!'

The blue eyes flicked over her, swift and cruel as an arctic wind. 'Let it be a lesson to you, Miss Mortimer. Never begin what you're not prepared—or equipped—to finish. Now, you mentioned something about my having robbed you. That's not only a slander, but a lie. I did my damnedest to talk your father out of the whole thing, but he wouldn't hear of it. He called it a calculated risk—I called it madness.'

'But you still went ahead and loaned him the money.'

'Yes,' he said. 'Because he might have pulled it off. By all accounts, he'd dragged Mortimers back from the brink more than once. If the Chinese deal had come off, I'd have been repaid, at a handsome rate of interest. Why should I have turned him down?'

'But you can't really want this house,' she said, almost feverishly. 'It's been in our family for generations. It's old-fashioned, and a nightmare to heat, and staff and keep clean. It's probably got woodworm, and dry rot, and—and deathwatch beetle.'

'No,' he said. 'Although it needs a certain amount of renovation and improvement, it's basically sound. Your father had a survey and valuation done not long ago—at my behest, naturally,'

'So you always recognised the possibility . . .'

'That your father might not be in a position to repay me? Of course.' He gave a slight shrug. 'Although I couldn't predict the present tragic circumstances, of course.'

'Of course," she echoed bitterly. 'And how long

do we have, Mr Bristow, before you start to recoup your losses by putting Ladymead on the market?'

'Oh, I'm not going to sell it,' he said casually. 'I'm going to live here.'

CHAPTER TWO

'LIVE HERE?' Alison repeated the words almost mechanically, her brain seething. 'You can't be serious!'

'I'm perfectly serious. It's a very charming house—or did you think only members of your own family had the taste to appreciate it?'

'Of course not.' She shook her head in bewilderment. 'But this isn't a very fashionable area—and a fair distance from London, and the kind of lifestyle you're accustomed to.'

Nicholas Bristow's mouth curled. 'How do you know the kind of lifestyle I'm accustomed to?' he asked flatly.

Alison flushed. 'You don't exactly keep your haunts—or your companions—a secret,' she said in a constricted tone.

'Ah.' He gave her a long look. 'I wouldn't have put you down as a devotee of the gutter press, Miss Mortimer, but let it pass. If you feel entitled to some explanation, then I'll give you one. I've a comfortable house in Town, but I've never regarded it as home particularly. Perhaps I've reached a stage in my life where the idea of putting down some roots has suddenly become appealing—I don't know. Anyway, people commute to City offices from far greater distances than this, and besides, there's room in the grounds for a helicopter pad if I thought it was necessary. Does that satisfy your curiosity?'

'It wasn't simply curiosity,' she said quietly. 'I'd

hoped, you see, if you were going to put the house on the market, to perhaps come to some arrangement, but I see now that's impossible.'

His brows rose. 'What did you have in mind, as a matter of interest?'

Her flush deepened burningly. 'I have a job. I thought, given time, I might be able to pay off the mortgage.'

'I doubt whether either of us would live long enough to see that happy day,' he said sarcastically. 'May I know what your salary is?' She told him, and he sighed. 'Miss Mortimer, this is the real world, not some fairy tale. It would take every penny you earn, and considerably more besides, and leave you with nothing to live on. I don't think any house is worth such a sacrifice, do you?'

'I don't think you understand. This is our home, and has been for generations . . .'

'I understand perfectly. But the reign of the Mortimers was coming to a halt anyway. Unless you or your sister plan to persuade your future husbands to change their names to Mortimer to carry on the old tradition?'

'I wasn't thinking particularly of Melanie or myself,' Alison said in a low voice. 'But being turned out of her home will be incredibly hard on my mother. She—she isn't very strong . . .'

'So I gather.' There was no softening in his face. 'I shall try and make sure she receives every consideration. Or did you think I was going to evict her bodily into some convenient blizzard?'

'I don't know what I thought,' Alison said wearily. 'But I do know that nothing you can say or do will cushion this kind of blow, especially following on from my father's death.'

'If your father had lived, he would have been

bankrupt,' Nicholas Bristow said harshly. 'I can't think that would have appealed to her either. In the present circumstances, she can leave Ladymead with dignity, and an income to maintain her, although it won't pay the upkeep of another house of this size,' he added, rather grimly.

'I think I've managed to work that out for myself,' Alison said bitterly. 'The fact is, Mr Bristow, you saw this house and wanted it, and that's why you won't consider any alternatives.'

'Unless you plan to come into a fortune, Miss Mortimer, there are no alternatives,' he said. 'But let me assure you that my dealings with your late father will remain private. As far as the outside world is concerned, I am in the process of purchasing Ladymead from your father's estate, as it's now too large for your family's needs.'

'Please don't expect me to be grateful.' Alison's chin lifted.

'No, I think I wrote off that possibility from the moment you entered this room,' he returned grimly. 'Next time you want to ask favours, Miss Mortimer, a softer approach might stand you in better stead.'

'I don't plan to approach you again for any cause whatsoever,' Alison snapped. 'Goodbye, Mr Bristow.'

She went straight to her room and threw herself across the bed. She wanted to scream and cry, and beat the mattress with her bare fists, but she was beyond tears. After a long time she sat up slowly, staring around her at all the dear familiar things which had surrounded her since childhood. Nothing stayed the same for ever, she knew that, but she hadn't expected the changes in her life to be so sudden, or so far-reaching.

Presently she would have to go downstairs again, to be at her mother's side when the bad news was broken to her, but first she needed to think—to consider practical possibilities, so that she could make some positive suggestions about how they could put the pieces of their lives together.

And, if she was honest, she needed a breathing space before she could face Nicholas Bristow again.

Alison's nails curled into the palms of her hands. This room no longer seemed a sanctuary for her. Already, his presence seemed everywhere. It made her writhe to remember him sitting on the edge of her father's desk, master of all he surveyed. He'd lost no time in making himself at home, she thought with angry bitterness.

But she had to admit that her suggestion that she might be able to buy back the house somehow had been a ridiculous one, prompted by a sense of sheer desperation.

She curled up against the pillows and began to think. Without her housekeeping duties at Ladymead to take into account, she could accept Simon's offer of full-time work, she thought, and the increase in salary, plus her mother's annuity, would allow them a reasonable standard of living.

She sighed soundlessly. Only Catherine Mortimer wasn't used to reasonable standards. She'd been indulged and spoiled all her married life, with every expensive whim catered to. She would not take kindly to any reduction in her level of spending.

And the other major problem was Melanie's school fees. She was being considered, Alison knew, as a possible Oxford entrant, and it was imperative for her education not to be disrupted.

But the cost of maintaining her at Mascombe Park was formidable.

Even if Simon were to make her a partner, she would still only be able to afford a percentage of the cost, Alison thought forlornly. It was late in the day to start thinking about scholarships, even if there were any available. Yet Mel deserved her chance.

Reluctantly Alison uncurled and stood up. Problems were building up like storm clouds, but there was no way to avoid in the inevitable cloudburst, or even postpone it.

She held her head high as she went downstairs.

'Well, I think the sooner we leave Ladymead, the better,' Alison spoke with quiet determination.

'But where can we go?' wailed Mrs Mortimer. Alison noted with compassion that her mother's hands were shaking. Yet during that long painful confrontation in the study, she had behaved with amazing control and dignity, listening without comment as the situation was outlined to her by a clearly embarrassed and unhappy Alec Liddell.

Nicholas Bristow had had little to say too, she recalled, his dark face almost sombre as he listened. She wondered if he had been feeling any kind of compunction.

She said, 'I'll talk to Simon when I go back to work on Monday, and see what he suggests. I know there's nothing very suitable on the books at the moment, and he might advise renting somewhere for a time.'

'Rented property?' Mrs Mortimer couldn't have sounded more anguished if Alison had suggested a tent in the middle of a ploughed field.

She sighed. 'I don't see what other choice we

have. You surely don't want to remain here on Nicholas Bristow's charity?'

'I can't imagine what he wants with a house like this,' her mother said bitterly. 'It's far too large for a bachelor.'

'I don't suppose he's going to be a bachelor for much longer,' Melanie, who had been sitting staring listlessly into the fire, roused herself to say. 'There've been heaps of stories in the papers lately about him and Hester Monclair. They reckon when her divorce goes through, they'll be married. She's divorcing her husband for unreasonable behaviour, and he's considering cross-petitioning for adultery, citing Nick Bristow.' She giggled. 'That'll stir up this village!'

'Melanie!' Her mother spoke with sharp disapproval, her mind diverted momentarily from her own troubles. 'Where in the world did you learn all those distasteful things?'

'One of the women who cleans the dormitories brings in her Sunday papers for us,' Melanie said promptly. 'She says it's only right we should know what wickedness there is in the world.'

'Well, I think I shall write to Miss Lesley when you return to school.'

'Don't you mean "if"?' Melanie muttered, but in too low a voice for her mother to hear. Alison shot her a warning glance.

'Mr Bristow's personal affairs are no concern of ours,' she pointed out. 'The least we can do is leave him in peace to conduct them. And that means finding somewhere else to live as quickly as possible.'

'But where are we going to find with sufficient room to accommodate us?' Mrs Mortimer demanded. 'There's the grand piano to consider, for one thing.'

Alison controlled a swift surge of impatience. 'None of us plays the piano, Mother,' she said gently. 'I think it would be better to let it go to auction.'

Mrs Mortimer's back straightened in outrage. 'May I ask, Alison, if you're determined to make me live in squalor?' she demanded.

'I'm not making you do anything, I hope— except maybe face a few facts,' Alison said wearily. 'We have to accustom ourselves to things being very different in future.'

Mrs Mortimer's eyes filled with tears. 'Aren't you beeing a little insensitive, Alison? I'm sure I need no such reminder.' She pressed her hand- kerchief to her lips, while her daughters exchanged despairing glances. After a pause, she went on, 'Hugh and Beth have very kindly asked me to stay with them, while I consider my future. I may well take them up on their offer. Now, I'm going to lie down for a while, and try to recover some of my strength. I presume dinner will still be served in this house this evening, Alison?' And on this, she swept from the room with a certain majesty.

'Mummy's brought making people feel guilty to a fine art,' Melanie remarked dispassionately when they were alone. 'I think that's probably why Daddy never confided in her about the mess he was in. He knew she'd make it a hundred times worse.'

'Don't say that, Melly.' Alison gave her a wry look. 'This must have been the worst week of her life. She loved Daddy very much, you know.'

'Yes, but she never helped him.' Melanie put another log on the fire. 'If he'd asked her to economise, she wouldn't have known what he meant. He couldn't—lean on her when the going got rough. I don't suppose she even knew he'd been having chest pains for months.'

'No, but then neither did I,' Alison said quietly, wincing a little.

'He probably thought you had enough on your plate already.' Melanie began to fiddle with the handle of the poker. She said suddenly, 'This is going to be my last term at Mascombe Park, isn't it?'

'The honest answer is, "Probably",' Alison admitted after a pause.

'I guessed.' Melanie's face was mournful. 'I suppose I could try and get a place in the local comprehensive, although the course will probably be different. Or would it be more help if I tried to get a job?'

'No.' Alison shook her head positively. 'You're Oxbridge material, Mel. You can't give that prospect up without a struggle.'

'I don't want to.' Melanie gave a faint grin. 'But something tells me that if we can't manage the fees, Miss Lesley will give me up without a struggle all right.'

'There used to be bursaries and things,' Alison frowned. 'I suppose we could enquire.'

'Mm.' Melanie gave a slight grimace. 'It would be hateful, though, going cap in hand. I'm not sure I wouldn't rather leave.'

'Well, don't let's make any hasty decisions,' said Alison. 'Mr Liddell's coming back tomorrow to talk over a few things, and I'll see what he has to say.' She hesitated. 'I would have mentioned it earlier, but I don't want to discuss personal family things in front of Nicholas Bristow.'

'You really don't like him, do you?' Melanie gave a little sigh. 'I think he's amazing! I wish I was Hester Monclair, lucky bitch. Of course she's gorgeous-looking, and sophisticated, and she probably knows exactly how to turn him on in bed . . .'

Alison was surprised into unwilling laugher. 'Mel, for God's sake! Don't let Mummy hear you.'

'Don't worry, I won't.' Melanie put her head on one side. 'But don't you fancy him, Ally? If you're honest, in your heart of hearts, just a little? You can't really prefer boring old Simon.'

'Simon is neither boring nor old,' Alison said calmly. 'And I wasn't aware that my sexual preferences—or Nick Bristow's for that matter—were on the "A" level curriculum. Stick to Eng. Lit.—it's safer.'

'What's safe?' asked Melanie, getting restlessly to her feet. 'We're all going to be living dangerously from now on.'

With her world visibly crumbling around her, it was a relief to Alison to find that the office hadn't changed. And nor had Simon, who seemed endearingly pleased to see her. The locality had been buzzing with gossip since the funeral, Alison knew, but Simon, with noble tact, refrained from asking any questions about the disposal of Ladymead.

He simply said that a smaller, more convenient house was vital, and promised to keep his eyes and ears open for suitable properties coming on to the market.

She was glad to be back at work. Melanie had returned to Mascombe Park, although for how much longer was anyone's guess. Alec Liddell had pursed his lips ruefully over the question of school fees, and when Alison had attempted to discuss the problem with her mother, Mrs Mortimer had dissolved into floods of tears.

It was not an attitude which helped, Alison thought tiredly, as she looked through an assortment of bungalow details. But then her mother's behaviour generally was giving her deep cause for concern. She wasn't eating, and hardly ever left her room. Alison had tried to persuade her to take up the Bosworths' invitation, although she supposed, privately, it was a rotten trick to play on Aunt Beth, but Mrs Mortimer wouldn't hear of it. She seemed to have it fixed on her mind that if she ever left Ladymead, it would be for ever, and Alison knew that the doctor was as worried about her state of mind as she was herself. He had started talking in guarded tones about the possibility of treatment in a complete change of scene, and the sound of it made Alison's heart sink.

'Are you saying my mother needs to see a psychiatrist?' she had asked.

Dr Barnet had given her a straight look. 'She's clearly in a very disturbed state,' he had returned. 'Bereavement is usually enough of a trauma for anyone to cope with, but when you add the other losses your mother is suffering . . .' He shrugged. 'Frankly, it's enough to undermine the emotional constitution of someone with three times her strength. And, unfortunately, she's become fixated on this house as a symbol of her security rather than you or Melanie. It's not a healthy situation.'

He could say that again, Alison thought, shoving the bungalow details back into their folders with scant respect. Nicholas Bristow had said he wouldn't evict them—but the way her mother was reacting, he might have to.

'It's my home,' her mother kept reiterating. 'My

only home. He can't take it away from me!'

The fact that they could no longer afford to live there seemed to have escaped her completely, Alison thought wryly.

She was thankful to have her work to immerse herself in once again, and she and Simon had already tentatively discussed the terms by which she would work for him full time.

It was a relief to know she would have a wage she could live on, but it didn't solve Melanie's problem, as the letter she had received only that morning served to underline. Melanie had had a preliminary interview with Miss Lesley, her formidable headmistress. It had been relatively civilised, Mel wrote, but the question of where the next term's fees would be coming from had inevitably been raised.

And that was the problem in the forefront of Alison's mind as she drove her elderly Mini back to Ladymead that evening.

As she rounded the last bend in the drive, she was surprised to see another car parked outside the front door. She didn't recognise the number plate, she thought frowningly, as she switched off her engine and got out, and she certainly wasn't expecting visitors.

As she walked into the hall, Mrs Horner appeared. 'It's that Mr Bristow,' she said in an undertone. 'He's been here over an hour. Asked for you specific, and not for madam, so I made him some coffee and hope I did right.'

'Quite right,' Alison said promptly, her spirits plummeting. 'Is he in the drawing room?'

'He is, miss. I told him madam wasn't too well, and that you were at work, but it made no difference. Said he'd wait.'

'Oh?' Alison returned wanly, as she unbuttoned her jacket.

He was standing by the fireplace, one arm resting on the mantelshelf, as he looked broodingly down into the flames. His head came round sharply as Alison closed the drawing room door.

'You're late, Miss Mortimer,' he remarked impatiently. 'I didn't know your work included overtime.'

'It doesn't as a rule.' She dropped her jacket over the back of a chair, aware of the disparaging glance he sent her plain navy dress. 'Just as I was leaving, my boss called me back to say he'd heard about a cottage that might suit us.'

'Oh.' He didn't appear to receive the news with ill-concealed delight. In fact, he frowned slightly. 'Where is this place?'

'Far enough away for us to be able to avoid each other,' she returned composedly.

His lips tightened. 'I see. And have you made an offer for it.?'

'Hardly. My mother and I have to see it first.' Alison touched the coffee pot and grimaced. 'This is cold. May I offer you some fresh?'

'No, thanks,' he said. 'But I'd sell my soul for a large Scotch—it's been one hell of a day.'

She gave him a surprised look under her lashes as she turned to get his drink. She was probably imagining things, but he seemed almost ill at ease.

'And you'd better have one too.' His voice followed her. 'You may need it.'

She poured a measure of Scotch into a glass and handed it to him. 'No, thank you. I've managed to cope so far without propping myself up with alcohol.'

'My congratulations.' He raised his glass in a

parody of a toast. 'You're clearly not as fragile as you look. I hope you can overlook the weaknesses of lesser mortals.'

'Admitting to weakness?' Alison asked sweetly. 'How very uncharacteristic!'

'Make the most of it,' he drawled, his eyes glinting. There was a brief silence, then he said abruptly, 'I didn't intend to come here in person. I was going to approach you through Alex Liddell in the first instance.'

She stared at him, suddenly dry-mouthed. She said huskily, 'I suppose you want us to leave.'

'No, on the contrary . . .'

'You've changed your mind? You're going to let us stay here?' Alison's heart leapt in joyous incredulity as she stared at him.

He frowned again. 'I'm afraid it's not as simple as that. A few days ago I contacted Liddell, and told him I would prefer it if the present staff continued working for me, if they were willing. I mentioned I'd like to meet the housekeeper for a preliminary chat.' He paused again. 'I must confess his reply staggered me.'

Alison sat down. 'He told you I was the housekeeper?' She shrugged. 'There's no problem, Mr Bristow. I can guarantee I won't take you to the industrial tribunal for firing me, and hiring someone else.'

He said abruptly, 'Isn't this formality rather overdone? My name is Nick.'

'To your friends, perhaps,' she said coolly. 'But you'll never count me in that small and exclusive company. I prefer formality.'

'As you wish,' he said coldly. 'But it imposes additional difficulties on the proposition I'm about to put to you.'

Alison's brows shot up. 'You're not offering me the job of housekeeper, I hope?'

'Yes, I am,' he said shortly. 'And before you turn me down, perhaps you'd better listen to the whole deal.'

'You think any deal on earth could persuade me to be your servant?' Alison asked dazedly. 'My God, you have some gall!'

'Listen to me,' he said impatiently. 'If you agree to what I want, you can have the lot. The house as your own, a self-contained flat for your mother—anything you wish.' He hesitated, then added flatly, 'And I understand from Liddell that your sister's school fees are a problem. I'll pay them, and see her through university too, if she makes the grade.'

Alison got to her feet. 'I wouldn't have any more Scotch,' she said sarcastically. 'You're obviously not well.'

He gave a short derisive laugh. 'In other words, I'm either drunk, or out of my mind! I'm neither, I assure you. I've thought it all out very carefully, and it seems to me to be an ideal solution to a number of mutual problems.'

'I think a good domestic staff agency would be an even better solution, and cheaper in the long run.' She began to move towards the door, but he came after her and took hold of her arm, halting her.

She tried angrily to shake herself free. 'Let go of me!'

'When you've heard me out,' he said inexorably. 'Sit down, Alison.'

'There's no point in my listening to any more of this. I have no intention of becoming your servant!' She stared at him in hostility and defiance.

'I'm not asking you to be a servant,' he said. 'Actually, I'm asking you to become my wife.'

There was a long pause, then Alison said shakily, 'You really must be—insane.'

'On the contrary, I'm perfectly sober, and in my right mind.' He pushed her back on to the sofa. 'Will you just listen for two minutes? I want this house to be run with the kind of calm efficiency I've noticed on each of my visits, and in spite of the fact you look about sixteen years old, I now know this is all your doing. But it doesn't stop there. I also need a hostess—someone used to entertaining—someone to accompany me in public when necessary. In other words, I want a wife.'

'Then I'm sure there's a whole queue of willing ladies only too happy to accommodate you,' she said stonily. 'Why pick on me?'

'If I wanted romance—passion—all the usual ingredients, why indeed?' His voice was ironic. 'But I don't. I want the practical advantages of marriage without the emotional involvement. And if you agreed to marry me, that's the kind of arrangement it would be.' His brows rose at the sound of her little indrawn breath. 'Or did you by some chance think I might have fallen madly in love with you?'

'No,' she said tautly, 'I didn't.'

'Then we've achieved one level of understanding at least,' he observed sardonically. 'Think about it, Alison. Your old home, and comfort and security for your family, in return for continuing to run this house, and acting the part of the dutiful wife in public.'

'I think marriage to you is a high price to pay, even for total security,' she said quietly.

'But as I've tried to make clear, it wouldn't be a

marriage in any real sense,' he pointed out impatiently.

'I understand that.' Alison shook her head, aware of a growing feeling of unreality. 'But would you really be content with such a cold-blooded arrangement for the rest of your life?'

'If I thought for one minute I was capable of finding the kind of genuine happiness my parents enjoyed, then probably not.' Nick Bristow gave a faint shrug. 'But that isn't going to happen. And I'm certainly not interested in saddling myself with declarations of undying love, and the inevitable tantrums when the thing comes unstuck. I know damned well what an ephemeral thing eternal passion is, at least where women are concerned.'

'Are men any different?' Alison asked steadily. 'Perhaps you've just been unfortunate.'

'Maybe.' He shrugged again. 'I'm in no real position to judge, but among my own friends I've seen any number totally committed to their marriages, and unable to see that their devoted wives are already looking over their shoulders, waiting for the next well-heeled idiot to come along so they can play change partners.' His mouth curled slightly. 'That isn't what I want. And I can't see why you and I shouldn't reach some kind of bargain which would satisfy us both.' He paused, the blue eyes measuring her. 'As an extra incentive,' he said, 'I know of someone who might be interested in buying your father's works as a going concern, instead of letting it fall into the hands of the receiver.'

'How wonderful to be able to exert such influence,' she said quietly. 'I only wish my future wasn't going to be part of all this wheeling and dealing. It tends to have an unsettling effect.'

The dark face held impatience. 'What reassurance can I offer? If you want a written contract, then I'll have one drawn up. You can impose whatever safeguards seem good to you. A mutual guarantee, if you like, that we won't interfere in each other's lives.'

'In other words, I'm not to enquire too closely into where you go, or what company you keep,' Alison said scornfully. 'I find that a revolting idea!'

'I can't see why any extra-mural activities of mine should affect you at all,' he said cynically. He paused. 'Unless, of course, it's you that has fallen madly in love with me.'

'Nothing,' she assured him, 'could be further from the truth.'

'That's what I thought,' he said drily. 'So why introduce emotional hassle into what is purely a business arrangement? If I were offering you any other kind of job, you wouldn't be probing into my moral rectitude.'

There was a kind of brutal truth in that, she was forced to admit.

'At the risk of probing further,' she said, after a brief hesitation, 'I thought there was a lady in your life already—someone you planned to marry, when it was convenient . . .'

'You mean when her divorce became final?' He studied Alison's responding flush with open mockery. 'I'm afraid you're under a misapprehension, my dear. And so is the lady, as I've had to make clear to her. She'll be far better off staying with her husband. He may be dull, but he stands to inherit a baronetcy.'

Alison's eyes widened indignantly. 'Isn't that rather callous?'

'It might be,' he agreed, 'if I'd helped to put her marriage on the rocks on the first place. As it happens, I didn't. Nor do I appreciate her throwing my name to any tame gossip columnist she had hanging round.' The firm mouth hardened into implacability, and in spite of herself, Alison shivered. 'I have no intention of being dragged into the Monclairs' current bout of mud-slinging, and finding myself an alternative bride without delay will help to snuff out any further speculation in that quarter.' He smiled faintly. 'As you see, the favours work both ways.'

Alison ran the tip of her tongue around her drying lips. 'If you want simply to be engaged—on a temporary basis—then maybe . . .'

'I don't,' he interrupted. 'I've told you my terms. I want a real engagement, to be followed in due course by a conventional wedding—although I suppose I'll have to spare you the white lace and orange blossom,' he added, his eyes flicking over her dismissively.

'Thank you,' said said grittily. 'But I don't need to be reminded that I fall far short of the usual image of the radiant bride.'

'Perhaps,' he agreed, without a single sign of repentance. 'But it wasn't any possible short-comings of yours I was considering, but the fact that you're still mourning your father. I think, in the circumstances, we could be forgiven for a small quiet wedding.'

It was all moving too far too fast, and she held up a hand. 'I—I can't answer you now. I must have time to think.'

'As you wish.' He paused. 'But without wishing to exert undue pressure, I'd be glad to have an answer by the end of the week at the latest.' He produced a card from a wallet, and handed it to her. 'My business and private numbers,' he said. 'I'll be waiting for your call.'

She couldn't think of anything to say in reply to this, at last managing a feeble 'Goodbye' as he walked towards the door.

'Let's make it *au revoir*, shall we?' She thought she could hear faint amusement in his voice. 'Because I'll be back.'

She was still trying to work out whether that was a promise or a threat when she heard the distant thud of the front door closing.

And, suddenly and uncontrollably, she began to tremble.

CHAPTER THREE

IT was a very long evening. Alison made herself have a meal, although she could not afterwards have stated with any accuracy just what she had eaten. All she could think of was Nicholas Bristow, and the amazing—the incredible offer he had made her.

At first, she told herself that it was all some weird dream from which, at any moment, she would awaken.

But the card with his telephone numbers printed on it was no figment of her imagination, even though she couldn't envisage herself ever dialling either of them.

She tried to look at his proposition in the same dispassionate way as he had made it, but it was impossible. Even if, as he'd promised, all they were to share was a roof and a name, the prospect was still a disturbing one, fraught with obvious pitfalls.

On the other hand, the chance of being able to achieve some kind of security for Mel and her mother was a tantalising one, which was why, she thought wryly, he had mentioned that aspect first. He knew her priorities, as well as he apparently knew his own.

Yet that didn't mean she was prepared to sell herself—for Ladymead, and the place in the sun it represented, she thought, staring sightlessly into the fire. Yet now it was back within her grasp, could she bear to let it go?

She moved restlessly. It was the sheer—

impersonality of the offer that chilled her, she had to admit, as she recalled the cool indifference of the blue eyes as they had glanced at her. Not that she wanted him to fancy her, she made haste to remind herself. But at the same time, it was hurtful to recognise the image he had of her as some boring, submissive, domesticated doormat. A born spinster, she thought savagely, only too eager to grab at any matrimonial opportunity to come her way, however unlikely or unrewarding.

Well, what a shock he'd get when she turned him down!

'I'm off now, miss.' Mrs Horner popped her head round the door. 'And madam's awake, and asking for you.'

'I'll go up right away.' Alison stirred guiltily. 'Did she have any dinner?'

'Cook did her a nice piece of steamed fish, and a little egg custard. She managed most of it,' Mrs Horner assured her. 'Good night, Miss Alison.'

Mrs Mortimer was propped up by pillows, her face set in lines of strain.

'That man was here,' she greeted Alison, as her daughter came through the door. 'What did he want?'

'Just to talk.' Alison sat down on the edge of the bed and took her mother's hand. 'How are you this evening? You were asleep when I peeped in earlier.'

Mrs Mortimer dismissed this with an irritated shake of her head. 'What does he have to talk to us about?' she demanded agitatedly. 'God knows we're at his mercy. I suppose he wants us to leave here. Well, I'll die first!' She began to cry again. 'This is my home, and it's too cruel for him to turn me out like this. Too cruel!' She began to thrash round on her pillows, making little moaning noises.

'Darling, don't,' Alison said gently. 'He didn't come here for that at all. In fact . . .' She stopped.

'What?' Her mother's fingers tightened almost convulsively round hers, hurting her. 'What did he want, Alison? Has he changed his mind about living here, after all? Is he going to leave us in peace?'

Alison shook her head reluctantly. 'He can't do that.' She paused. 'Mummy, Simon told me about this cottage today. It's at High Foxton, so you could still stay in touch with all your friends. It sounds really quite nice, and we could just about afford it. Would you like to see it?'

'No!' Mrs Mortimer's eyes were alarmingly wild and bright suddenly. 'I'll never leave here—never! This is my home, not some squalid cottage. We must buy Ladymead back. Your Uncle Hugh might have the money. We must ask him to help us.'

'Darling, you can't,' Alison said firmly. 'Uncle Hugh has responsibilities of his own, and I shouldn't think he could lay his hands on even half the amount Nicholas Bristow would want. Even if he'd sell—which I doubt.'

'I thought perhaps that was why he'd come here. To offer to sell the place back to us.' The look of hope in her mother's eyes was almost more than Alison could bear.

'No,' she said with a sigh, 'It—it wasn't that. He came to offer us—a share in it, I suppose. On certain conditions.'

'A share?' A share in Ladymead?' Mrs Mortimer drew a long quivering breath. 'In our own home?'

Alison sighed silently. 'But it isn't ours any longer,' she said patiently. 'You have to come to terms with the fact that it belongs to Nick Bristow now, lock, stock and barrel. That's why it would be so much better to get away from here and start again.'

'How can you say that?' Her mother's tone was harsh with reproach. 'This is the house where you were born. Oh, you're so hard, Alison. I sometimes wonder how you came to be any child of mine.'

'As you've often told me,' Alison said wryly. She got up. 'Get some more rest now, Mother. We'll talk again tomorrow.'

'No, now.' Mrs Mortimer's fingers fastened like manacles round Alison's wrist. 'Tell me about this offer of the Bristow man's. Does it really mean we can stay here? What conditions?'

'He wants me to—work for him in a certain capacity.' Alison chose her words carefully.

'Work?' her mother echoed. 'But a man like that would already have all the staff he needs, surely. He could pick and choose, and you aren't even trained for anything.'

'I don't think there's much formal training for the kind of job he's offering,' Alison returned drily. 'And it's staff for Ladymead that he's looking for.'

'But Alec Liddell assured me that Cook—Mrs Horner—everyone would be kept on. Are you telling me they're going to be turned out too?'

'On the contrary, he's anxious for the *status quo* to be preserved when he takes over. I imagine he would find any form of domestic inconvenience profoundly irritating.'

'Then what's the problem?'

Alison shrugged, striving for lightness. 'The problem is he's discovered from Alec that I've been—running things for you since I left school, and he wants me to go on doing so.'

Mrs Mortimer levered herself up against her pillows, her attention sharply fixed on her daughter's face. 'He wants you to keep house for him—and we can live here while you do?'

'Yes.' Alison looked down at the carpet. 'Ridiculous, isn't it?'

'Ridiculous? It could be the answer to our prayers!' There was excited colour in Mrs Mortimer's face, and she looked more animated than she'd done for weeks, Alison realised with a pang. 'What did you tell him? Did you agree?'

Alison shook her head. 'Not yet. You see—there's more.' She hesitated, then said baldly, 'He wants to marry me.'

'Marry you?' Mrs Mortimer slumped back in genuine if unflattering astonishment. 'Nicholas Bristow wants to marry you?' She shook her head. 'Darling, it must have been some strange kind of joke. He can't have been serious!'

'That's what I thought,' Alison agreed, refusing to allow herself to be wounded by her mother's immediate assumption that she could have no charms for a man like Nick Bristow. After all, it was no more than the truth, and she knew it, and to allow even one pang of hurt was merely being stupid. 'But I have until the end of the week to give him my answer, so that seems to indicate he means business.'

'Good God,' Mrs Mortimer said faintly. There was silence, then she said, 'What are you going to say?'

Alison's brows lifted. 'No, of course. You couldn't expect me to agree to such an outrageous proposal. He—he doesn't care for me. I think I could do better for myself than be married as a convenience.'

'Do better than Nicholas Bristow? Are you quite mad?' Mrs Mortimer sat up energetically, grasping her daughter's hands in hers. 'Alison, he's offering you your home back—your heritage. That's what you must think about. And there's Melly to consider.'

'I know,' Alison acknowledged. 'She was part of the package, as a matter of fact.' She tried a smile. 'Oh, all the strings were gold-plated, and designed to appeal. No wonder he's such a success in the City!'

'Then how can you even consider refusing?' Mrs Mortimer demanded.

Alison's chin came up. 'Daddy sold himself to Nick Bristow,' she said with terrible clarity. 'Are you seriously suggesting I should do the same thing?'

'But this may be his way of trying to make amends to us,' her mother said eagerly. 'Alison, for God's sake—at least consider!'

Alison looked at her incredulously. 'You—really mean it?'

'Of course I do!' Mrs Mortimer thumped the coverlet with her fist. 'For heaven's sake, darling, be rational. You're far too sensible to be carried away by dreams of some overpowering romance. It just isn't going to happen, and instead you're being offered the chance to recover everything we've lost, together with the kind of husband most girls would be fighting over,' she added a shade waspishly.

'Perhaps that's part of the trouble,' Alison said drily. 'Maybe I'd prefer a man who wasn't quite so universally attractive.'

'Now you're being absurd.' Mrs Mortimer released her hands and threw herself back on her pillows. She was looking agitated again. 'Alison, you can't do this to us! It would be too selfish to deliberately reduce us all to penury, when it could all be so different—and just for a few silly scruples. I feel that Nicholas Bristow is doing his utmost to behave honourably in this—dire situation. And the last you can do is meet him halfway.'

'The least?' Alison didn't know whether to laugh or cry. 'To sell myself to a man I hardly know just for security? To give up my own life—the possibility of a career . . .?'

'A career!' Mrs Mortimer almost snorted. 'I suppose you mean working for a pittance at that estate agent's. And if you're imagining for one minute that Simon Thwaite will have any further interest in you once we've lost Ladymead, then think again, because the Thwaites have always married money.'

'And Simon will know his duty, even if I don't.' Alison bent her head. 'Thank you for being so frank. It's just as well I'm not in love with him.'

'If you were, naturally I would exert no pressure, but in the circumstances . . .' Mrs Mortimer retrieved a lace-edged handkerchief and dabbed at her mouth. 'Alison dear, it isn't given to us all to fall deeply in love as I did with your father. Very satisfactory relationships have been known to evolve from very little.'

'But how do you build on nothing at all?' Alison asked ironically. 'It will be interesting to find out, I suppose, if nothing else.' She pushed her hair back from her face. 'Uncle Hugh said Daddy was a gambler; I must be more like him than I thought.' She bent and dropped a light kiss on her mother's hair. 'Don't look so worried, darling, you're going to have your way. Ladymead will be restored to us, with all the other fringe benefits. I'll phone Mr Bristow now and tell him, before I lose my nerve.'

She went down the stairs slowly, clinging to the banister rail as if she was afraid her legs would crumple and betray her. She'd left Nick Bristow's card beside the phone, and it lay there, staring up at her, forcing her to respond—to act.

Alison swallowed, running the tip of her tongue over achingly dry lips, before reaching for the receiver and dialling his home number.

It was strangely appropriate, in the circumstances, that it was an answering machine, and not Nick himself, that replied.

She waited for the tone, then said colourlessly, 'Mr Bristow, this is Alison Mortimer. I've considered your proposal, and the answer is—yes. Good night.'

When she replaced the receiver, her breathing was as harsh and hurried as if she'd taken part in some marathon race.

A pretty antique mirror with a gilt frame hung above the telephone table. She looked at herself steadily, registering her pallor, and the wide, frightened eyes under the delicately winged brows.

Aloud, she said, 'Well, it's done, and somehow I have to live with it—and make the best of it.' Then she turned away.

She awoke in the night to find tears on her face, feverish with dreams she could only remember in part. She fetched herself a glass of water from the bathroom and lay in the dark sipping it, and listening to the rain on the window, wondering restlessly whether Nick Bristow had played back the tape on his machine yet. She bit her lip. Of course, she was taking it for granted that he would be spending the night under his own roof, although she had no real reason to suppose he would be.

It was far more likely that he would be with one of his ladies. If not Hester Monclair, then someone else, she thought with distaste, then immediately chided herself. She had no grounds to speculate now, or at any future time about that side of his life. He'd made that very clear. He would live his life, and she would live hers, and on the occasions when their paths crossed, she would be expected to keep to safe, neutral topics of conversation.

That, after all, was part of the price she was going to pay for Ladymead, and her family's security.

She grimaced, drinking the rest of her water, and settled back with determination, willing herself back to sleep. But it wasn't as easy as that. In the darkness, she kept seeing Nick Bristow's image, almost as if he'd been etched on to her aching eyes.

'This is ridiculous,' she muttered crossly, turning over and burying her face in her too-hot pillow. She was tired and worried and confused, that was all. That was why she was having these adolescent fantasies suddenly about how it would feel to have that hard, cynical mouth touching hers in passion, or see something more than indifference in those cool blue eyes.

Alison groaned aloud, and dealt the inoffensive pillow a blow with her clenched fist, telling herself restlessly that it was more or less inevitable that the wretched man should be on her mind. After all, she'd only agreed to marry him a few hours before.

But if she had to think of him, why did it have to be in such blatantly physical terms? It certainly wasn't like her. Simon had held her in his arms, and kissed her, but he'd never managed to intrude upon her dreams, sleeping or waking.

She'd thought she'd woken in tears because she'd been thinking of her father, but now, she was not so sure.

Yet there was a logical explanation for everything, she told herself severely. Nick Bristow was a shatteringly attractive man, quite apart from the cataclysmic effect he had had on her life. It was little wonder, surely, that he was preying on her mind.

But once this strange business-marriage of theirs was a *fait accompli*, things would change, she decided resolutely. Her role would be to run Ladymead in the same ordered groove as always, and Nick Bristow would hardly impinge on her life at all. That was the way they both wanted it, after all, and that was the way it would be.

She overslept the next morning, and was having a hasty breakfast with one eye on the clock when she heard the sound of a car coming up the drive. It was too early for visitors, she thought, grabbing her bag as she rose to her feet. Her mother was still asleep, and Mrs Horner would have to fend off whoever it was.

As she reached the dining room door, it opened abruptly, and Alison stopped with a little gasp of surprise as Nick Bristow strode in.

She had never seen him wearing anything but formal clothes, but this morning he was casually dressed in close-fitting black denim pants, topped by a rollneck cashmere sweater in the same colour, and a suede jacket slung over one shoulder.

He said without preamble, 'I got your message. I thought we'd better talk—finalise things.'

'Oh?' Alison gave him a hostile glance, aware that her pulses were still drumming haphazardly. Why had he had to pop up like the Demon King? she wondered crossly. 'Well, I'm afraid I have other plans for today.'

'Then cancel them.' His tone brooked no opposition. 'Ring work, if that's where you're going, and tell them you won't be in. Say you're ill, if you prefer our engagement to remain our little secret for the time being,' he added sardonically.

She set her teeth. 'I was going to work, yes. I have a busy morning ahead, and as it happens, I was going to ask my boss if I could have the afternoon off to be with my mother. She hasn't been at all well and . . .'

'I'm aware of that. Perhaps the news that she doesn't have to move out of this house will be just the tonic she needs. And I've had to postpone today's schedule too. I thought we'd drive over and see my mother. I think our respective families should be the first to know the good news, don't you?'

'Good news?' Alison gaped at him. 'You talk as if this engagement was real!'

'As far as the rest of the world's concerned, it is.' Again a note in his voice forbade argument. 'You're almost bound to confide in your mother. As she'll be living under the same roof with us, she's sure to realise we're not enjoying a conventional relationship. But I'd prefer my mother to retain some illusions. Although she'll be so relieved that I'm answering her prayers at last that she won't enquire too closely, but welcome you with open arms.'

'Oh, really?' Alison lifted her chin. 'I'd have said

I was the last girl on earth she would ever expect you to produce as her future daughter-in-law.'

Nicholas shrugged. 'That's a risk we'll have to take,' he dismissed. 'Now, phone your boss, and let's make a start.'

It was foolish, she knew, but his failure to utter even a token reassurance about her suitability rankled with her.

She said stiltedly, 'My mother is still in her room, but I'm sure she'll want to—speak to you . . .'

'To assure herself about my prospects?' The dark brows lifted mockingly. 'Well, there's no problem. You were going to offer me dinner here, I hope.'

Alison was taken aback. 'Yes—if you wish.' The thought of spending the entire day in his company, and the evening as well, was a frankly disturbing one.

He smiled rather grimly, as if he had gauged her inner turmoil. 'I feel we should further our acquaintance, don't you?'

She shrugged slightly. 'Perhaps. I had the impression we wouldn't be together a great deal.'

'Yet we can hardly be expected to shun each other this early in the relationship.' He sounded amused, and slightly impatient. 'I'm paying highly for your services, Alison. I expect a little co-operation.'

She avoided his gaze. 'Yes—well, I'll go and make that call.'

She told Simon she was involved with some unexpected business concerned with her late father's estate, and accepted his sympathetic enquiries like soothing balm for her feelings.

A sleek black Porsche was waiting for them on

the drive, and Alison's brows rose. 'No driver today?' she asked sweetly.

'I thought privacy was more important,' Nick retorted, opening the passenger door for her. 'You'll have to trust yourself to my tender mercies.'

And how! Alison thought silently as she adjusted her seatbelt.

'You don't waste words do you?' Nick Bristow observed after they'd travelled the first few miles in silence.

'Sometimes,' she returned coolly. 'But you're hardly here today for the pleasure of my company.'

'True.' His mouth curled slightly. 'But as I've already pointed out, part of the bargain outlined to you was that you should "play the part" of my wife. Maybe you should begin by rehearsing the role of the happy fiancée. Hard looks, and answering me in monosyllables, are hardly going to convince anyone that we're the victims of a mutual and overwhelming passion.'

'I didn't know that was the impression I was supposed to give.' Alison stared rigidly ahead of her. 'If that's so, perhaps you should get yourself a better actress.'

'Or perhaps you could make more effort,' he retorted on a note of exasperation. 'For God's sake, Alison, this isn't easy for me either.'

She flushed. 'I'm sorry. But I'm sure we'd find it—simpler, if I were just the housekeeper.'

'For you, perhaps,' he said sardonically. 'Unfortunately, my requirements extend beyond the purely domestic, as I've already made clear to you. You knew that when you telephoned me last night, so why are you having second thoughts now?'

'Because of something called the cold light of day,' Alison said wryly. 'I'm just beginning to realise what I've got myself into. And your attitude isn't helping to reconcile me to my fate either.'

'I apologise.' He shot her a lightning glance. 'But I didn't think you'd welcome any—overt demonstration. Do you want me to make love to you?'

'Not if you were the last man on earth,' she said huskily. 'That isn't want I meant, and you know it. You complain about me, but you're barely civil yourself.'

Nick glanced in his mirror, then swung the car off the quiet road on to the verge.

'Then I must apologise again, and this time I mean it,' he said quietly. 'I think we're both going to have to make a number of allowances that we never bargained for, but even if our relationship isn't quite what we may have originally envisaged for ourselves, there's no reason why it can't work perfectly well.'

'I don't know.' Alison stared down at her hands, tensely clamped together in her lap. 'Are you sure you've thought it through? All the implications?' She took a deep breath. 'Children, for instance.'

He gave a faint frown. 'Perhaps I'm lacking in the paternal spirit, but I've never had any wish to see any little carbon copies of myself running about.' He studied her, his frown deepening. 'Although I admit I hadn't looked at the problem from your point of view. Perhaps, if things work out between us, in a few years we could consider adoption.'

She said wearily, 'Perhaps,' and discovered to her chagrin that she wanted very badly to burst into tears.

She fought it, and said with an assumption of calm, 'And there's one other thing I think we should get straight. I've heard a lot about the way you intend to—conduct your private life when we're married. Can I take it that I'm entitled to the same amount of leeway?'

'What the hell are you talking about?' She'd set him back on his heels for once, Alison noted with satisfaction. He couldn't have looked more amazed if she'd suddenly grown a second head in front of him.

'I'm sure I don't have to go into details,' she said sweetly. 'Or do you expect me to live like a nun?'

'No, of course not,' he denied impatiently. 'Although I admit I hadn't considered . . .'

'That I was enough of a woman to have any emotional needs of my own?' she asked flatly.

'Don't put words into my mouth,' he said harshly. 'Let's say I hadn't credited you with that kind of sophistication. My impression was that you were sexually innocent, but I've been wrong before.'

'We're not discussing what I am, but what I may become,' Alison said calmly. 'I can't live on the fringe of your life, and remain totally unscathed. And perhaps my lack of experience is just lack of opportunity,' she added with bravado.

He said between his teeth, 'If it's experience you want, sweetheart, then I'll be only too happy to oblige you.'

She heard the click as her seatbelt was released, then Nick pulled her towards him with such force that her little cry of protest and outrage was stifled on her lips.

His dark face seemed to swim before hers, and instinctively she closed her eyes to blot him out, only to experience instead the first ravaging assault of his mouth on her own.

His hand clamped at the back of her head, forestalling any movement of rejection, forcing her to accept his kiss, his lips grinding hers bruisingly against her teeth, as he sought to impose a deeper intimacy.

She couldn't move. She could hardly breathe, but she fought him silently, her aching mouth tightly compressed against his invasion. Her hands were pinned helplessly between their bodies, and she could feel beneath her palms, disturbingly, the warmth of his skin through the thin sweater, and the hurry of his heartbeat.

Then, as suddenly, she was free, drawing shaky gulps of breath into her lungs as she shrank back into her seat. A couple of buttons on her shirt had become undone during the brief fracas, but she was damned if she was going to start fumbling to fasten them while he was watching her, she thought stormily. Her hair was standing on end too, and she probably hadn't a scrap of lipstick left.

'Disappointed, darling?' His voice was soft and goading. 'Sexual skirmishing not all it's cracked up to be?'

'Is that what it was?' Alison lifted her shoulders in a faint shrug, thankful that her voice, at least, sounded composed. 'I have been kissed before, actually, but with rather more finesse.'

'You amaze me,' he drawled. 'And I hope you responded with rather more finesse too. I'd say you had a lot to learn before taking your place as a woman of the world.'

'Probably,' she said. 'But with luck, I'll find a more considerate teacher.'

'I wouldn't count on it,' he said softly. 'And I'd better warn you now that after we're married, I expect you to behave with discretion.'

'Isn't that what they call a double standard?' Her lower lip felt tender, and she touched it tentatively with her finger.

'Call it what the hell you like,' he said tersely. 'I can't stop you amusing yourself, but I won't allow you to flaunt your affairs in my face either. You'd better remember that when you start looking round for a lover.'

He paused, as if waiting for some reply, but when none was forthcoming, simply shrugged, and re-started the car.

It took the remainder of the journey for Alison to regain some semblance of her normal quiet composure. It hadn't been a kiss, she thought, seething. It had been rape in miniature, and he knew it as well as she did. And if that was a sample of what other women flocked round him for, then they must be insane!

That strange inner trembling had, thank goodness, subsided by the time Nick parked in front of a pleasant red brick house, set back from the road in what looked to be extensive grounds. If she was nervous now, it was for a very different reason. She got out of the car, and stood taking deep breaths of cool air.

'Relax.' Nick took her arm, and she had to fight the impulse to pull violently away. 'She won't eat you—you're what she's been dreaming of for years.'

Nick's mother was slight with a mass of grey-streaked dark hair, and eyes as vividly blue as her son's. But that was where the resemblance ended. Mrs Bristow's eyes were alight with joyous pleasure, her smile as wide as the world as she welcomed them.

'This is wonderful!' She hugged Alison almost fiercely. 'When Nick phoned almost at dawn and said he had a surprise for me, I never guessed what it was. You wicked pair! Why didn't you give me a hint? I haven't even a bottle of champagne to drink your health.'

'I didn't want to arouse your hopes,' said Nick. 'After all,' he added, with a sardonic glance at Alison, 'she might have turned me down.' He watched the swift colour flood her face, and laughed. 'You see—she actually blushes! I'd forgotten women could.'

'You've been moving in the wrong circles, darling.' His mother gave him a fond but minatory smile. 'But you've seen sense at last, thank the Lord. I'm so relieved that . . .'

'I'm sure you are,' he broke in drily. 'Now why don't you offer us some sherry in place of the undoubtedly tactless reminiscence you were about to favour us with?'

'Oh, I'm sure Alison has few illusions about you, my pet,' Mrs Bristow said serenely. 'Women rarely do, you know. And what they say about reformed rakes is true, you know. Your father, bless him, was proof of that.' Her smile grew misty for a moment, then she rallied. 'Now—that sherry.'

Lunch, prepared and served by a plump and beaming elderly soul who turned out to have been Nick's nanny many years before, was delicious, and it should have been a happy family celebration, but Alison was on edge the whole time.

She would, she thought ruefully, have found it easier to take if Nick's mother had eyed her askance, and made her aware she fell well short of requirements. To be welcomed so completely and affectionately was almost more than she could bear.

After lunch, Mrs Bristow suggested a stroll round the garden, and Alison accepted eagerly. Gardens were neutral territory, and herbaceous borders a safer topic of conversation than personalities.

But she hadn't bargained for Nick accompanying them, or less still for the casual slide of his arm round her waist as they walked along. It was simply part of this charade they were acting, and she knew it, but she couldn't repress the deep, responsive shiver that went through her as he drew her lightly against him.

It was normal. It was what anyone would expect of an engaged couple, but, oh God, it was so hard to accept, she thought miserably as she made herself listen to what her future mother-in-law was saying about buddleia.

At last Nick looked at his watch. 'I think we'll have to tear ourselves away, love. But I'll bring Alison over to see you in a few days and you can talk weddings. We've decided on a quiet family affair in the circumstances.'

'You wouldn't rather wait a little?' his mother suggested.

He shook his head determinedly. 'No, Alison's been through a hell of a lot lately. I want to have the right to take care of her as soon as it can be arranged.'

'Of course you do.' Mrs Bristow smiled at them both. 'You'll have some tea before you set off? I'll go and see about it.' She hurried off, leaving them to follow at their own pace.

The silence between them was almost tangible, and Alison felt it needed to be broken.

She said, 'What a lovely garden this is. Surely your mother doesn't do all of it herself?'

'She does as little as I can arrange,' Nick told her. 'I employ a full-time gardener for her to bully.' At her enquiring look, he explained, 'Her heart isn't all that strong. She pooh-poohs it, but she needs to avoid undue exertion. Even having me was something of a risk, which is why I was an only child.'

'Oh, I'm sorry.'

'You don't need to be,' he said briefly. 'She leads a very full life, actually, now that she's adjusted to widowhood.'

Alison found herself wondering whether her own mother would eventually do the same. It was very early to tell, of course. Nick's mother had had time to recover and rebuild her life. And the two women were, of course, very different personalities.

Nick's voice cut across her reverie almost prosaically. 'I'm afraid we're under observation from the drawing room. We'd better not disappoint her.'

Before she had realised what he meant, he had stopped, drawing her into his arms.

He said quietly, 'Don't fight me this time, Alison.'

The sun was warm on her upturned face. Somewhere near at hand a bird sang with piercing sweetness. She could not have moved even if she'd wanted to do so. And she didn't want to.

That was the last coherent thought she produced before his mouth came down on hers. He was very gentle, very restrained, acting the kiss, but in fact barely brushing her lips with his. And suddenly, shockingly, it wasn't enough.

Suddenly, Alison wanted to be closer. She wanted to press herself against him, to draw him down to her, to open her mouth to his intimate exploration. She wanted the kiss to be real, born of a need which refused to be denied, instead of this cool travesty of an embrace which hardly even acknowledged the fact that she was a woman.

She felt her nails dig into the palms of her hands in endurance, and as if he sensed her sudden tensing, Nick lifted his head.

'Don't panic,' he advised acidly. 'Your ordeal is over.'

Until the next time, Alison thought, walking beside him, her heart banging against her ribs like a terrified bird. Until the next time.

CHAPTER FOUR

IT was a very simple dress, Alison thought. Made of crêpe in a shade somewhere between grey and lavender, it relied for its effect on the elegance of its cut, and details like the full sleeves falling to tightly buttoned cuffs, and the deep white collar. It certainly didn't look like a wedding dress. But then she didn't feel like a bride.

She put up a hand and smoothed back a tendril of hair. Melly had done her proud, she thought with a faint smile, swirling the soft brown cloud into an elegant topknot, and securing it with the spray of matching flowers which had come with the dress and which she hadn't quite known what to do with.

But Melly had known. In fact, Alison thought with a sigh, it was a pity she was the younger sister. If the positions had been reversed, Melanie would have coped ebulliently with everything— especially Nick, with whom she flirted out- rageously, considering him as her future brother- in-law, fair game for her to practise her wiles on.

He encouraged her, of course. With Melanie, Nick was more human than Alison had ever seen him, except perhaps with his mother—teasing, affectionate and endlessly indulgent.

And entirely different, she had to admit, from the way he behaved towards herself.

She grimaced slightly. Well, what did she expect, after all? The bargain between them was made, and legally signed under the bewildered aegis of Alec Liddell. And Nick had been generous—that she could not deny, even if she wanted to. She had been astounded by the size of the personal allowance he was making her, in addition to the account he had opened at a local bank for the payment of all the household bills. He had made it clear such mundane details were to be left to her. What he had concerned himself with was the redecoration of the house. Alison found herself spending evening after evening poring over portfolios of sketches and designs, and swatches of fabric and wallpaper. Her initial resentment of the clean sweep he was making in what had been her family home was soon outweighed by the realisation that refurbishment was badly needed and had been for some years.

Her mother, however, was not so easy to convince, and there had been a number of near-clashes between them, with her sweetly-voiced reproaches on one side, and Nick's scarcely veiled intolerance on the other. Fortunately, he had produced a master-stroke by inviting her to choose exactly how she wanted her own flat, converted from a little-used guest suite overlooking the rose garden, designed and decorated, and Mrs Mortimer was soon happily absorbed in her own plans, and less inclined to dwell mournfully on what she called 'change for change's sake'.

For herself, Alison had found little to quarrel with in Nick's taste, and they had achieved a reasonable harmony. The only awkwardness had arisen when he had shown her the designs for their respective bedrooms. She had not realised until then that he intended to use the master bedroom and the adjoining room for their accommodation, and had protested instinctively.

Nick looked at her, his brows lifting coldly. 'I

realise, of course,' he said, 'that you'd like me banished to the other end of the house, or even to a separate building for preference, but I'm afraid the next room is as much concession as I'm prepared to make. I've already told you—as far as outsiders are concerned, this is a normal marriage.'

She swallowed weakly. 'But there's a communicating door . . .' she began, intending to tell him that the adjoining room was intended principally as a dressing room.

'How incredibly suggestive,' Nick drawled, giving her a contemptuous look. 'Would you like me to have it bricked up? Or would a bolt on your side only be adequate?'

Her face had burned with mortification, and she'd mumbled, 'Perfectly adequate,' before turning away and picking up some samples of curtain fabric with hands that shook, and studying them as if her life depended on it.

In the circumstances, she had decided ruefully, it would be downright dangerous to query why Nick had opted to install a king-sized bed in her room instead of something more appropriate and conventional.

Mrs Mortimer was going to stay with the Bosworths, after the wedding, and the decorators would be moving in during the month that Nick and Alison would be away on honeymoon.

Alison sighed. The honeymoon had proved to be another bone of contention. She had considered it an unnecessary refinement, until Nick's mother had raised the subject.

'Where are you taking Alison, darling?' she had asked cheerfully. 'Somewhere glamorous and exciting, or quiet and restful?'

'A little of both, I hope,' Nick had returned

lightly. 'I've chartered Greg Parsons' yacht to cruise the Greek Islands.'

At the small surprised sound he had startled out of her, he had turned to Alison solicitously. 'What's the matter, sweetheart? You don't suffer from seasickness, do you?'

If she'd had her wits about her, she would have replied firmly, 'Terribly', and that would probably have been the end of the matter. But she was too astonished and indignant to be able to think clearly.

As he drove her back to Ladymead later, she had rounded on him furiously. 'You didn't tell me we were going on honeymoon!'

'It's the usual course of action after one's married,' he returned casually. 'What's the matter? Do you have some objection?'

'Any number,' she retorted. 'Isn't it carrying things rather to farcical extremes?'

'On the contrary, it's a perfectly conventional thing to do,' Nick drawled. 'And as I'm tired of telling you, on the surface at least, this is going to be a very conventional marriage. But if you have some rooted aversion to the Greek Islands, then I'll tell Greg we don't want his boat after all.'

'I think my rooted aversion is rather closer to home,' Alison said clearly and coldly.

He smiled thinly. 'I'd rather managed to work that out for myself. I'm afraid you'll just have to grit your teeth, darling, and keep reminding yourself that nothing lasts for ever in this uncertain world. Once the honeymoon's over, I'll do my best not to intrude too much on your halcyon little world down here. For whole periods at a time you should be able to forget that I exist at all.'

If only she could believe that! Alison thought bitterly, as she stood on the steps at Ladymead and watched the tail-lights of the car vanish.

One of the most disturbing facets of her brief, hectic engagement had been how completely Nicholas Bristow had managed to brand himself across her consciousness. She supposed it had been unavoidable in the circumstances. There were so many arrangements to be made, so many details to be agreed, even on a mundane level.

And, once she was legally his wife, would things really be any different? And now that her quiet existence had been turned irrevocably upside down, would she be content to stay at Ladymead waiting for his visits, like—like some dreary Mariana of the Moated Grange?

She looked restlessly round her room. It was odd to think she would never sleep here again. The next time she came to Ladymead she would have to use the enormous room which Nick was having decorated for her in shades of ivory and aquamarine, and sleep in that bed—as wide as the Gobi Desert, and as barren, she thought with sudden bitterness.

Oh God, how had she allowed herself to get involved in this wretched mess? She wanted to hide. She wanted to crawl back into her own narrow bed, and pull the covers over her head, and say she was ill, say she was—anything, as long as it meant she wouldn't have to drive with Uncle Hugh to the Parish Church and become Nicholas Bristow's unwanted bride.

And at that moment heard a tap on the door, and her uncle asking anxiously, 'Are you ready, my dear? It's time we were leaving.'

'Coming!' she made herself say. Then she picked

up the prayer-book her father had given her at her confirmation, and went to the door.

His face lightened at the sight of her. 'You look lovely, child,' he declared with false heartiness.

She smiled at him, knowing that neither he nor Aunt Beth could comprehend why she was taking this step. They'd been stunned when she first told them the news, then overtly disapproving, then resigned. In fact, Aunt Beth had thawed sufficiently to make her niece a private gift, in addition to the exquisite Georgian writing desk which had been their official wedding present.

Alison hadn't known what to expect when she untied the ribbons on the silver and white striped box, and hadn't known whether to laugh or cry as she had inspected the contents—several sets of the most exquisite handmade lingerie she had ever seen—satin and crêpe-de-chine trimmed with lace in shades of ivory, oyster and coffee—a tacit acknowledgement, she thought drily, that Aunt Beth considered she would need every weapon in the armoury to hold her husband's interest. But what Aunt Beth never would—never could know was that it was a battle which would never be fought. She'd left the lovely things in their box in her wardrobe.

She was surprised to find how crowded the church was as she moved up the aisle to the voluntary. She supposed the announcement of her marriage had been something of a nine-day wonder locally. She was glad to see a number of familiar faces from Mortimers. It still wasn't certain what was going to happen to the works, but it looked as if it was going to be saved, or so Nick had told her rather curtly when she had timidly enquired. His intervention seemed to have been successful.

But Simon wasn't there. His reception of the news that she was to be married to Nicholas Bristow had made her wonder whether her mother's assessment of him had been justified. It had clearly hit him hard, and Alison hadn't known whether to be glad or sorry. Glad, she supposed, because there had been one man who had actually wanted her for herself. Sorry, on the other hand, because she knew she would never have returned his feelings.

She realised with a start that the music was swelling to a crescendo, and glanced up into the cold hard glitter of Nick's eyes as he waited for her at the chancel steps.

His face was mask-like, but he was angry. She knew it—could feel it. But why? Was he disappointed, perhaps, that she had not opted for the white dress and the veil after all? Yet that had been the agreement—no formal dress, family only, and a tiny reception at her uncle's house afterwards.

She was no beauty, of course, but he'd known that from the beginning, so it was hardly fair to blame her for it now.

And for appearances' sake at least, he might have smiled at her. She wanted him to smile. She wanted to put up a hand and touch his face, stroke away the harsh lines beside his mouth, and the fierceness of that wanting sent a shock like an electric current through her entire being.

In an agony of relief, she switched her attention to the kindly, familiar figure of the Vicar, and the words he was beginning to say to them. Obediently she repeated what she was told to say, put out her hand to receive Nick's ring when obliged to, but all the time her mind was whirling in small, frantic circles.

The tension of the last weeks had finally got to her. She was cracking up. That was the only feasible explanation for that piercing rush of feeling. And a fine way to embark on marriage—as a hopeless neurotic.

She was amazed how soon it was over, how soon she was walking back down the aisle, but on Nick's silent arm this time. The silence followed them into the car, wrapped them round as they drove the few miles to the Bosworths' house. Nick showed no inclination to break it, and Alison didn't know where to begin. Perhaps they would never exchange another word for the rest of their lives, she thought, a little hysterical bubble of laughter welling up inside her.

She was glad Aunt Beth had prepared a buffet lunch, instead of a formal meal round the long mahogany table in the dining room. That way, she could pretend to eat and no one would notice.

There was only one couple at the reception she hadn't met—Nick's cousin Judith, and her husband Alan.

'Welcome to the Bristow clan,' said Judith, her eyes fixed on Alison in candid assessment as they shook hands. 'You look pole-axed!' she added with a grin. 'I remember it had much the same effect on Alan when it happened, and I'm much less formidable than Nicholas!'

'Don't you believe it,' her husband put in. 'We should have met before, Alison, so that I could have talked you out of it. You're clearly far too nice a girl to fall into the clutches of a hardened reprobate like Nick.'

Alison joined in the general laughter, forcing the muscles of her face to smile until they ached. They were being kind, but she could sense the astonishment underneath. They were wondering why the wealthy, glamorous Nicholas Bristow had saddled himself with such a nonentity, when he could have chosen almost any woman he wanted. They were his friends as well as relations. They moved in the same social circles in London. They would know his usual girl-friends—be aware of what he looked for in his women. And for the life of her she could think of no feasible explanation which would satisfy them.

Even her mother had adapted to the new situation with the speed of light. She had stopped calling Nicholas 'that man' from the first day of the engagement, and had in fact behaved as if the whole thing was a love match engineered by herself in some way. Alison sighed inwardly. Her mother had decided that long fraught encounter between them had never happened, it seemed. And how nice it must be to be able to ignore reality when it became inconvenient!

And reality was here and now in the shape of Melly, telling her that it was time she went up to change.

'Are you going to leave your hair up?' Melanie asked as Alison carefully took off her wedding dress and began to put on the soft coral silky two-piece she had chosen as her going-away outfit.

'I don't think so.' Alison smiled rather carefully as she fastened her zip. 'It was a nice effect for the occasion, but now I think I'd better revert to being me again. And it's very much casual clothes and relaxation on the cruise. He—Nick—stressed that,' she added, aware of how difficult she still found it to say his name. '*I, Alison Mary, take thee, Nicholas . . .*'

Melanie sighed luxuriously. 'The Greek

Islands—how truly envy-making! It'll be perfect now—all those wild flowers.'

'Yes, it should be lovely,' Alison agreed with deliberate neutrality.

Melanie picked up her wedding dress and began to replace it on a padded hanger, her face pensive. She said suddenly, 'Ally—you are happy, aren't you? It's all been so sudden and—miraculous, from my point of view anyway, with Nick stepping in like this and taking over all our lives. I suppose I've just taken it for granted that it's what you want too. But it is, isn't it?'

'Of course.' Alison unpinned her hair and began to brush it with smooth rhythmic strokes back into its usual shining neatness.

'Thank heavens!' Melanie hung the dress on the wardrobe door, and spent a few minutes arranging and rearranging the folds of the skirt. She said suddenly, 'I'm really sorry I said all those bloody stupid things about Nick—and all that stuff in the paper. There was probably nothing in it, you know. In fact in Sunday's paper, it said that Mrs Monclair had gone back to her husband, and they'd had a complete reconciliation, which proves it, doesn't it?'

The note of appeal in the last question wasn't lost on Alison. She smiled at her sister. 'Of course it does,' she said soothingly. 'But then I never did believe any of it anyway.'

'That's good.' Melanie beamed at her. 'Are you wild about him? You must be. It's a bit like a fairy tale, isn't it?'

Alison transferred her star sapphire engagement ring back to her left hand, reluctant to face any more of this eagerly artless interrogation. Let Melanie enjoy the romance she had conjured up in her imagination. She only hoped disillusionment would not come too soon.

The *Ariadne* was moored at Rhodes, so Nick had informed her, and they were spending the night at a hotel not too far from the airport prior to taking an early flight the following day.

The first hurdle, Alison thought, as she waited in the luxurious foyer for Nick to register. He'd been as taciturn as ever on the drive to the hotel, merely asking if she was comfortable, and whether she'd like to listen to some music. She had let the stately strains of Vivaldi fill the space between them. What she would do if there was no piped music in the hotel, she had no idea.

Nick seemed to be taking a long time at the desk, and when he rejoined her, he was frowning thunderously.

'The suite I booked is not available,' he said curtly. 'Apparently some damned fool set fire to a waste paper basket, and the whole place has to be redecorated. Shall we find another hotel, or do you want to take what they have to offer?'

Alison gave a faint shrug. 'What's that?'

Nick's mouth curled in a mixture of wryness and derision. 'The bridal suite,' he said.

He saw the embarrassed colour wash into her face, and nodded. 'I thought as much. We'll find somewhere else.'

'No.' Alison caught at his sleeve as he turned away. 'We can make do with it, surely. It—it's getting late, and I'm tired.'

It was his turn to shrug. 'Then we'll take a look at it.'

When they were ushered into the suite, Alison's first wish was that they had gone somewhere else.

Someone had clearly lavished time and money on turning the suite into the perfect love-nest. There were red roses waiting in the small sitting room, beside a complimentary bottle of champagne on ice, but that was only the start of it. In the bedroom, the huge bed was covered in ruched apricot satin, and draped with filmy curtains in the same shade. And the sunken bath in the turquoise marble bathroom was clearly intended for dual occupation.

Alison had an overwhelming desire to laugh until she hiccupped. Only the certainty that Nick was certainly not sharing her amusement kept her silent. But at least there was a couch in the sitting room, she thought, and she'd noticed him noticing it too, so they could manage for this one night.

'Charming,' Nick remarked too pleasantly. He tipped the porter. 'Have our bags brought up immediately, please.'

As the door closed behind the man, Alison said defensively, 'Well, it will do.'

'It seems it will have to,' he said acidly. 'Shall we get into the spirit of the occasion by having some champagne?'

'Why not?' Alison moved towards the window, stumbling slightly as she did so. 'Goodness, this carpet is thick!'

'Wall-to-wall mattress,' observed Nick, opening the champagne.

She felt her face warm, and went on hurriedly, 'There isn't much of a view.'

'Obviously an unnecessary refinement,' he drawled. 'The occupants are supposed to have better things to do with their time than stare out of the window. Here's your champagne.'

She took the glass he handed her with a numb word of thanks.

'So what shall we drink to?' Nick went on. 'The usual matrimonial toasts seem a little loaded in content for our situation. Would "To our better acquaintance" be going too far, do you suppose, or shall we just say, "Cheers"?'

'Please, don't.' Alison stared unhappily down at the floor.

There was a silence, then he sighed. 'I'm sorry, Alison. I'm giving you a rough time, aren't I? Can I say I've found today more of a strain than I believed possible, and leave it at that?'

She nodded. She said constrictedly, 'I don't think it's been easy for either of us.'

He slid off his coat and put up an impatient hand to loosen his tie. 'It will be good to get on board *Ariadne* and unwind,' he said, half to himself. 'All in all, it's been a hell of a six months.'

A knock on the door heralded the porter with their luggage. Alison sat on the window seat and sipped her champagne and listened to Nick giving clipped instructions about newspapers, and an early call, and breakfast. As the porter left, he gave Alison a swift sideways glance.

Perhaps he was surprised they hadn't already been in some kind of clinch, she thought ruefully. Or, more probably, he was surprised that they were there together at all. Because she knew she didn't look like a bride. She didn't feel like one, either.

'Do you want to eat here, or go out?' asked Nick, glancing at his watch. 'There's a good restaurant on the river, not too far from here, where I can usually get a reservation.'

She could guess in whose company, and the thought cost her a nasty little pang. She said coolly, 'I'd just as soon eat in the hotel, thanks. As

I said, I'm rather tired.' She finished her champagne and got up. 'I think I'll have a bath.'

'Well, take care you don't drown in that monstrous thing,' Nick told her, pouring himself some more wine. 'Would you like me to show you how the jacuzzi works?'

'Good God, no!' Her voice was appalled.

The blue eyes mocked her. 'But you might find it—er—stimulating. It's time you started to live a little, Mrs Bristow.' He paused. 'And I was only suggesting a demonstration, not that I should share it with you.'

'Well, that's naturally reassuring, but I'm really not interested.' She managed to keep her voice equable, but inwardly she was in knots. He was doing it deliberately, she thought stormily, because he knew quite well that sharing a bath with a man was something totally outside her experience. That, and a great many other things besides. In fact, he probably thought she was left over from the Dark Ages.

She took her time over her bath, and wasn't altogether surprised when she eventually emerged to find she had the suite to herself. She couldn't blame him. The ambience of the place must be setting his teeth on edge. Yet if their relationship had been different, they might have enjoyed its absurdities together, she thought with a faint sigh.

She put on a sleeveless green dress and sat down to wait for him. When he returned, he seemed preoccupied again, but fortunately no longer interested in tormenting her.

They enjoyed a quiet, civilised dinner, then went for a walk in the hotel grounds, relishing the last freshness of the late spring evening.

When they returned to the suite, Alison felt

almost relaxed. During an earlier exploration, she had discovered extra blankets in one of the fitted wardrobes in the bedroom, and she brought an armful through to the sitting room and deposited them on the end of the couch, together with a spare pillow, for Nick to find when he came up from having his nightcap in the bar.

Then she went and got ready for bed, changing into a pair of the thin cotton pyjamas she preferred to nightgowns. She had brought a paperback novel in her case, a detective story by a favourite writer, and she managed a chapter before turning off the lamp and sliding down into that preposterous apricot cloud.

She was half asleep when she heard Nick come in quietly and go into the bathroom, and she closed her eyes with even greater determination, burrowing down under the covers. She heard him emerge at last, and waited to hear the bedroom door close behind him.

Only it didn't. She heard the sounds of movement in the shadowy room, a rustle, then the dip of the mattress beside her as Nick got into the bed.

Suddenly sleep was a million miles away. She shot upright. 'What do you think you're doing?'

'Trying to get some sleep,' he returned flatly. 'If you imagine for one minute that I'm going to spend my wedding night falling off some bloody sofa, you can think again, and fast!'

'But you said—you promised . . .' Breathing was difficult, articulation more so.

'And I meant it. I'm here for sleep, darling, not sex. God knows this bed would sleep twelve at a pinch, so there's no danger of any—close encounters in the night. Unless,' he added, 'you insist, which I doubt.'

There was a long silence. Alison didn't trust her voice to say anything.

'I thought not,' he went on, just as if she had spoken. 'One other thing—I should warn you, perhaps, I sleep in the raw, and always have done, but you seem to be wearing enough for both of us, so you can comfort your outraged modesty with that. Goodnight, Mrs Bristow.'

He turned on his side, punched his pillow into shape, and appeared to become instantly oblivious to her.

Lying wide awake, rigid with nerves and embarrassment, Alison savagely envied him his sangfroid. She stared into the darkness, listening to his quiet even breathing for a long time, then began slowly and cautiously to edge away from him, towards the furthest limit of the bed.

She was being foolish, and she knew it. Nick had showed no sign at all of wishing to pursue her shrinking body across this vast expanse of apricot satin, but she needed to get as far away from him as possible, just in case by some mischance she happened to touch him accidentally in the night. She moved cramped limbs cautiously, as she huddled on the edge of the bed. Because if she touched him, and he woke and thought she was— that she wanted ... She swallowed painfully. The consequences were too humiliating to contemplate even, and she dared not take the risk.

Her wedding night, she thought unhappily, and it promised to be the most uncomfortable, miserable night she had ever spent. She wanted very badly to cry, but knew she couldn't because, again, she might awaken Nick. She touched her clenched fist to her lips. It was irksome to realise just how accustomed he was to sharing his bed, she thought bitterly. He'd fallen asleep almost at once, whereas she would be fortunate if she closed her eyes all night.

But she was wrong. Eventually sheer physical and emotional exhaustion overtook her, carrying her into some deep twilight tranquillity, from which she emerged to find daylight filtering into the room through the pale curtains.

For a moment she was disorientated, wondering dazedly where she was, and whether she was still dreaming, then she turned over, stretching cramped limbs, and saw Nick, propped up on one elbow watching her, and reality came back with a jolt.

She said, 'Oh!' with a little gasp, and tugged hastily at the covers, a reaction which was acknowledged by his sardonic grin.

'Good morning,' he said. 'I've been lying here wondering whether this cruise is such a good idea after all. Perhaps you'd have preferred a mountaineering holiday. Are you a keen climber?'

Alison took a hasty gulp of breath and sanity. 'I've never done any rock-climbing in my life.'

'Amazing,' Nick said silkily. 'Judging by the way you've been clinging to the edge of this bed, I thought you must spend all your spare moments bivouacking on narrow ledges up the North Face of the Eiger.'

She gave him a muted glare. 'Well, you're wrong.' She made a performance of looking at her watch. 'What's the time? How long is it before we need to be at the airport?'

Nick said lazily, 'There's plenty of time.' But the growing speculation and amusement in the blue eyes nullified instantly any sense of reassurance Alison might have felt.

'Well, perhaps we should be making a move just

the same,' she found herself babbling, and he laughed.

'Stop pressing the panic button,' he advised coolly. 'What's the matter? Did your mother warn you that men are at their most dangerous early in the morning?'

'No.' It was no more than the truth. Mrs Mortimer's material advice had been restricted to a few embarrassed remarks about Nick being 'a man of the world' and girls being 'so much better informed these days, darling, than we ever were'.

He laughed again. 'Then perhaps she should have done,' he said.

Before she could escape, or take an evasive action, his arm was across her, imprisoning her, the weight of his shoulders pinning her to the bed. His mouth was warm and deliberate, and terrifyingly persuasive as he began to kiss her. The heat of his bare skin was penetrating the thin cotton pyjama top, making her tremblingly aware of her own helplessness and vulnerability. Her lips were already parting obediently to the insistence of his kiss.

This time he was neither forcing her nor playing a part, Alison realised dazedly. He was seducing her. As his mouth moved enticingly on hers, his hand was stroking her slender throat, marking the flutter of her pulse, before sliding down into the modest vee opening of her pyjama jacket. His fingers brushed gently across the upper curves of her slight breasts, and she felt the breath catch in her throat with shamed excitement. The touch of his hand on her naked flesh, the warm sensuous invasion of her mouth, were an almost painful delight to her untutored senses.

The sudden ringing of the telephone was like a

slap across the face, a rude awakening from the sensual dream world which had begun to enfold her.

Nick released her, snarling an expletive under his breath, and turned to pick up the receiver.

'Yes?' His tone was not encouraging.

The sound of his voice had an instant effect on Alison, rocketing her back to earth with a vengeance. A soundless gasp of dismay escaped her as she realised he'd undone half the buttons on her pyjamas without her even being aware of it. Clumsily, she tried to repair the damage, pushing aside the covers as she did so, and swinging her feet to the floor.

'Our early call,' Nick said shortly, replacing the receiver. The blue eyes appraised her burning face and shrinking figure, and his mouth curled slightly. 'Or I suppose you could say—saved by the bell!'

She was amazed to hear how steady her voice sounded. 'You promised you'd leave me alone!'

'I know,' he said. 'But the temptation to—coax you a little was quite overwhelming, believe me.'

'Really?' Alison asked coolly. 'I'd have said myself that it was because I—just happened to be there. A kind of reflex action on your part.'

His face darkened. 'You could be right,' he said after a brief pause. 'However, it won't happen again. You have my personal guarantee on that.'

'I'm not so sure that's a valid assurance,' she said bitterly.

The lines beside his mouth deepened harshly. 'It was an impulse, for God's sake—one which I now regret. Or did you think it was a deliberate plot, hatched by my lust-crazed brain?' he added contemptuously. 'God, you must think I'm desperate!'

'No.' His words were like a whiplash, but she bore them without flinching, at least not outwardly. 'And nor am I. Perhaps you'd remember that.'

'With pleasure.' Nick sat up with energy, pushing the covers away, and reaching for his robe, making Alison avert her gaze hastily. 'The instruction is now etched on my memory cells for ever. And you needn't worry about the *Ariadne*. She's a big boat. Play your cards right, and we need only encounter each other at mealtimes. Now, would you like first use of the bathroom, or shall we flip a coin?'

'No, I—I'll go first.' She couldn't bear to stand there any longer, confronting him over that great expanse of bed, like enemies on opposite sides of some vast sexual minefield.

She didn't care for the connotations of the bathroom either, but it seemed like a sanctuary, as she bolted the door behind her.

She was shaking all over suddenly, her heart racing madly, and she sank down on the tiled rim of the bath with a little stifled groan, thankful that Nick's piercing gaze could not pursue her here, and see the state she was in.

Or had he already guessed, she asked herself bleakly, just how close she had been to complete surrender?

She sighed. Nothing was working out as she had expected, least of all her own emotions. And that was the most troubling realisation of all.

CHAPTER FIVE

ALISON poured a measure of sun-oil into her palm and began to massage it into her neck and shoulders. Over the weeks, she had acquired a warm honey tan, and she didn't want to spoil everything by burning now—especially when, tomorrow, they would be on their way back to Rhodes, and home.

Home, she thought. Ladymead—redecorated, and refurbished, and waiting for their occupation. It was amazing how remote it seemed suddenly. Light years away from the gently swaying deck of the *Ariadne*, and the sunbed with its prettily striped awning set above it.

Surprising, too, how quickly these four weeks which she had so much dreaded had passed, and how easily.

After that first disastrous morning, she hadn't known quite what to expect from Nick. Further advances, possibly. Recriminations and resentment almost certainly. And yet it hadn't happened. Once they'd embarked on *Ariadne*, Nick had undergone some kind of sea-change almost in front of her eyes. On the flight to Rhodes he had been silent and aloof, deep in his own thoughts, and Alison had sat beside him, her normal nervousness due to the flight exacerbated by his remoteness. How could she spend the next month of her life imprisoned on a boat in the Aegean with a man who neither looked at her nor spoke? she wondered wildly. Anything would be better—even a flaming row.

And then, suddenly, everything had changed. Nick had gone to his stateroom on *Ariadne* a hostile stranger, and had emerged the next day a relaxed, friendly companion.

She had responded to his casual camaraderie shyly at first, and then with growing confidence as the days passed. And there was no denying that he had brought the islands of Greece alive for her in a way she could not have imagined. She had brought several excellent guide books, but he had taken them away from her, telling her she would learn far more by looking and using her senses to interpret what she saw. She hadn't realised before how well he knew the islands, and loved them, and he made her share his own enthusiasm, as well as teaching her to appreciate their variety of landscape and atmosphere.

She had scrambled with him over the ruins at Knossos, walked with a strange sense of awe beneath the stone lions on sacred Delos, caught her breath at the bleached beauty of Hydra, and giggled at the pompous pelican of Mykonos.

She'd swum, and sunbathed, and even, after some caustic coaching from Nick, tried her hand at water-skiing. She had acquired her tan, and even put on some weight, filling out the painful hollows in her collarbones and around her slender pelvis. She no longer felt selfconscious in her bikinis, which was just as well, because Nick, groaning with exasperation, had confiscated the one-piece suits she had brought with her.

'Enjoy the sun while you can,' he had dictated. 'You have a long English summer to face when we get back!'

Alison replaced the cap on her sun-oil bottle, and rolled on to her stomach, stretching her arms luxuriously above her head. It was no wonder she'd put on weight, she thought—all this good food and lazing about. The *Ariadne* might not be the largest boat in the Mediterranean, but a lot of money had been spent on ensuring the comfort of its passengers, and the amiably efficient crew included a first-class chef.

Not that they always ate on board, by any means. Some of the happiest times she had spent on this strange honeymoon had been in local tavernas, eating seafood, drinking the neighbourhood wine, and even joining hilariously in the inevitable dancing. She was still inhibited, but she was learning, she thought with a faint smile.

And Nick, she had to admit, had made it easy for her to do so. There had even been times over the past weeks when she had found herself wishing that this relaxed wandering from island to island might never stop—times when she had been conscious of their inevitable return to England like a cloud no bigger than a man's hand on her horizon. Because there would be problems. To begin with, there was no guarantee that her mother would accept her new role as little more than a lodger in her old home. Alison could foresee some stormy passages ahead as Mrs Mortimer began to grasp that Ladymead had a new master.

And the new master's attitude would be important too, she thought with a little sigh. If Nick could be as he had been with her for the past month, then everything would be simple. But the fear haunted her that he might revert to being a sardonic stranger again.

Alison bit her lip. Dealing with problems like this was, she supposed, all part of the price she had to pay for her family's security. But it explained why, for the first time in her life, she was almost reluctant to see Ladymead again.

She heard someone approaching, and looked up to see Nick coming along the deck towards her. He was wearing a towel knotted round his lean hips, and above it his skin looked like burnished teak. The sheer force of his attraction dried her mouth, and made her shake inside, much as she tried to fight it. She was glad that her sunglasses hid any possible betrayal in her eyes. She was also thankful that as he preferred to sunbathe naked, as he slept, he invariably chose a different section of the deck. His cool announcement of what he intended to do had provided one of the few awkwardnesses of the cruise, she recalled, yet in practice, as long as she remembered to keep to her own part of the deck, there had been no embarrassment at all. She sometimes wondered what the crew made of such an ill-assorted pair of newlyweds, but if they had any opinions, they were too well trained to let them show.

Nick squatted on his haunches beside her, running a measuring hand along her shoulder. 'Don't you think you've had enough sun for one day? I was going to suggest we got showered and changed, and went ashore for a farewell dinner at Yanni's.'

'That sounds fine.' His touch could not have been more casual, yet already it had had the effect of constricting her breathing, it galled her to realise. Fortunately, he did not touch her very often. 'But I think I'll have five minutes more here. According to that paper George brought on board yesterday, it's been raining all week in Britain.'

His mouth curled slightly. 'That has a certain

grim reality about it!' He paused. 'In fact, it almost makes me sorry we have to break out of this charmed life we've been enjoying, and face it all.'

It was startling to find that his feelings reflected her own. She made a performance out of reaching for the paperback she had been desultorily reading, and finding her place. 'Well,' she said lightly, 'all good things must come to an end.'

'So they say.' There was a curious note in his voice. 'And has it been good for you, Alison?'

'Of course,' she said rather stiltedly. 'It's been a revelation. I've never been to any part of the Mediterranean before. We tended to spend most of our family holidays in Scotland—my mother doesn't care for very hot weather.'

Nor, she thought, would Catherine Mortimer have liked the poverty, and the dust, and the basic facilities offered by the tavernas they'd visited. Plastic tablecloths and primitive plumbing were not her style at all. Alison hadn't realised until then that they were hers, either.

She went on carefully, 'I'd like very much to come back some day.'

Nick shrugged. 'It won't be this year,' he said flatly. 'I'm going to be too busy to consider another break.'

'Yes, of course.' Alison kept her gaze fixed on the printed page, vexedly aware that she was blushing again, although her sunwarmed skin would disguise the fact. The last thing she wanted was for Nick to think she was hinting for another expensive trip. 'So I'll just make the most of the time I have left,' she added too brightly.

'My sentiments exactly,' drawled Nick, getting to his feet. 'I'll see you later, then.'

When he had gone, Alison made no further

pretence of reading. She pushed the book away
and lay flat, her head pillowed on her folded arms,
getting herself back under full control again. She
was ashamed of her own reaction, she thought
angrily. She was behaving like an impressionable
schoolgirl. She had no illusions about Nick
Bristow—none at all, she told herself vehemently—
yet just because he had exerted himself to be
pleasant, to charm her a little, she was almost
eating out of his hand. It might have been safer if
Nick had remained the arrogant self she was
accustomed to; she would not have been so ready
to lower her guard.

Because that was all it was, she thought. The
enforced proximity, the isolation, and the
undoubtedly romantic surroundings had had their
own insidious effect on her.

She sighed a little. Perhaps, after all, it was just
as well they were going home soon.

Hours later, she was convinced of it. Yanni had
welcomed them back to his taverna with his usual
exuberance, and led them ceremoniously to their
special table, the candles already lit, and the ouzo
poured.

And tonight, he told them proudly, the
speciality of the house was lobster.

They ate it grilled, with a salad made from
tomatoes, cucumber, peppers and *fetta* cheese,
sprinkled with herbs and olive oil. It was a long,
enjoyable, and inherently messy meal, imposing its
own kind of intimacy on the occasion, and to
follow there was a dish of glossy purple grapes,
large as plums, resting on a bed of vine leaves.
And with the meal they drank the light, dry,
palatable wine of the locality.

'And so you are leaving us?' Yanni said. He gave Alison the look of passionate admiration with which Greeks like to gladden the hearts of women tourists.

'I'm afraid so,' she said ruefully. 'We shall miss coming here.'

'Po, po, po.' He clapped Nick on the shoulder. 'When you return, my friend, we shall be here, *né*? And bring your children to play with mine,' he added as an afterthought.

Nick returned some smilingly negligent answer, while Alison shrank back into the shadows, bitterly aware that her face was burning again. It wasn't the first such reference she'd had to contend with. At the wedding reception, Nick's mother had made a lighthearted remark about wanting to be a grandmother which, fortunately, only Alison seemed to have heard.

Nick was conferring with Yanni over the bill, and merely nodded when she murmured something about going on ahead.

The street leading away from Yanni's and down towards the harbour was steep and stony, and Alison picked her way with a certain amount of care, although there was plenty of illumination from the flanking houses, interspersed with tavernas, kafeneions and shops. Although it was still comparatively early in the season, the atmosphere in the village was busy and alive, and she lingered, looking at some of the souvenirs. She had bought things to take home, of course. The exquisite Cretan embroideries were already boxed up for her mother, and she had got a supple leather holdall for Melanie, and ceramics for Mrs Horner and the rest of the staff. But nothing for herself.

She looked at some silver ear-rings, then put them down again. She didn't need anything tangible to remind her of the events of the past month, she realised suddenly. They were all there—engrained in her mind for ever. She walked on down the hill, staring in front of her, seeing it all unrolling in her head, as if she had operated some mental switch—everything Nick had said. Everything Nick had done.

She stopped dead, with a little gasp, as all the implications of that came home to roost.

It was ridiculous, she thought frantically. He'd been—kind—friendly, that was all, and it had got to her a little. There was no more to it than that. There—couldn't be.

And any moment now he was going to come striding down the hill and find her standing in the middle of the street as if she'd been turned to stone.

A few yards away, the door to the little church stood invitingly ajar, and she made for it like a criminal seeking sanctuary.

It wasn't a wealthy village, but the church was bright with paint and gilding, the depiction of Christ in Majesty which surmounted the altar gleaming richly in the light of the many blazing candles. The scent of burning wax and incense was pungent in her throat, as she looked round her, instinctively drawing the wrap she wore up to cover her half-naked shoulders.

She wasn't alone, she discovered. There were two women, dressed in the conventional black with headscarves, standing beside the great bank of votive candles, and lighting others in supplication or thanksgiving—Alison could not be sure which.

She moved, her heels making a sharp sound on the wooden floor, and they turned and saw her, smiling at her shyly and gesturing her to draw closer. As she did so, one of them held out an unlit candle to her.

They thought she was there on the same errand as themselves, she realised, and how to explain that she was not without causing offence? It was altogether easier to take the proffered candle and light it from one of the others as they were doing, and add it to the blazing mass already assembled.

Swiftly she held it to the flame, watched it flare up, then placed it in one of the waiting wrought-iron holders. She was aware of approving nods and smiles. Aware too that they were crossing themselves constantly, and praying, their lips moving ceaselessly under the partial concealment of the scarves they wore.

She needed to say something too—but what? She stood blankly, watching the dancing flames—and heard a voice in her head, saying over and over again, *'Make him love me, oh, please, make him love me!'*

For a moment she thought she had spoken the words aloud, but there was no reaction from her companions, absorbed in their devotions, and presently she turned away sharply, and almost stumbled to the door, taking deep breaths of the night air as she regained the street.

Hands gripped her shoulders. Nick's hands. She straightened and tried to meet his searching gaze with an assumption of her usual collectedness, but her heart was thudding in her chest as if she had taken part in some marathon.

'What the hell is it?' he demanded sharply. 'Are you ill?'

Alison shook her head, moving away from him. 'It was—stuffy in there, that's all.'

'Why did you go in there?' he asked. 'Is it famous for something—icons, or frescoes, perhaps?'

'Nothing like that.' She moved off. 'I was just—curious.'

'I wondered where the devil you'd got to,' he told her. 'I got all the way down to the harbour, and George was waiting with the boat, but he said he hadn't laid eyes on you. I realised you'd been sidetracked, but I confess I would never have guessed the church.' He paused. 'Isn't it a little early to be renewing your marriage vows?'

The mockery was back in his voice with a vengeance! Alison stiffened. It seemed as if he was signalling that the honeymoon period between them was over.

'I was merely interested,' she said shortly. 'We've walked past it often enough. I wanted to take a look inside ... nothing to make a fuss about.'

'I wasn't aware I was making a fuss.' There was an edge to his voice. 'And there's no need to charge off like a maniac either,' he added sarcastically. 'The boat will wait for us, you know.'

Alison slowed reluctantly, biting her lip. She was completely thrown by what had happened back there in the little church. Perhaps she'd drunk too much wine, she thought, or was suffering some strange reaction to the lobster. People said that, sometimes, shellfish affected you. Somehow she had to rationalise that pathetic, urgent little prayer which had come from nowhere.

And, somehow, it had seemed essential to

distance herself from Nick, the author of all this emotional confusion.

Now she had to force herself to walk in silence beside him, her thoughts in turmoil.

She was overreacting, she told herself desperately. That's what it was. She was letting the moonlight, and the candlelit dinner they'd just shared, and Nick's undeniable sexual charisma, affect her.

She had thought she was immune, but now she knew she was not, and it was something she had to come to terms with. Something to beware of too.

And that would undoubtedly be easier to do back at Ladymead, where they would be leading virtually separate lives anyway. She shivered slightly, drawing her wrap more closely around her. She knew the terms of the bargain she had made with Nick. It had a black and white simplicity, so why, suddenly, did she feel so hopelessly confused?

George was waiting with the boat at the bottom of a steep flight of steps. They were narrow and slippery, but Alison had negotiated them without difficulty on a number of occasions. Yet this time, as she tried to step across into the boat, her foot slipped, and with a little cry she found herself falling helplessly forward.

Nick grabbed her, his arms like steel bands as he pinioned her against his body, her feet dangling ignominiously, her breathless face pressed into the curve of his shoulder.

For an endless moment Alison was powerless in his arms, her small breasts crushed against the hard muscularity of his chest. She could breathe nothing but the warm, clean scent of his skin—feel nothing except this agonising intimacy of contact.

Her startled fingers curled convulsively into bone and sinew, clinging like the claws of a kitten, as her whole being responded to his nearness with a long uncontrollable shudder of need and longing. She wanted to press herself closer still, experience the hardening arousal of his body against her slender thighs. She wanted to know that he shared with her this swift anguish of desire . . .

And instead, she felt herself set gently but firmly on her feet.

His voice quiet against George's more vociferous expressions of concern, Nick asked, 'Are you all right?'

'Yes, of course.' She put up a hand and pushed her hair back from her face, managing an artificial little laugh as she did so. 'I'm sorry, I'm not usually so clumsy. I must have had too much of Yanni's ouzo!'

'It's lethal stuff.' His agreement was casual almost to the point of indifference, as he released her and turned away, and Alison drew a deep breath of relief.

At least he hadn't known—hadn't recognised that sudden, shameful rush of feeling in her. She'd been spared that, at least. She sat silently in the bows and watched the solid bulk of *Ariadne* take shape out of the darkness. She couldn't wait to get back on board, she thought feverishly. It wasn't much of a refuge, but it was all she had.

There was usually coffee waiting for them in the saloon, and little glasses of the liqueur tasting of tangerines she had grown to like over the past weeks, but tonight these were pleasures she would forgo, she thought. Being alone with Nick was something she needed to avoid.

So she murmured some constrained excuse, and

made off to the solitude of her stateroom. And tonight, for the first time, she turned the key in the lock, her hand trembling slightly as she withdrew it from the door. She was being ridiculous. All these weeks it had never occurred to her to lock herself in, so why now?

As a safeguard, she told herself bitterly. An insurance against making a complete and abject fool of herself. Because that was the real danger.

She undressed swiftly, and showered in the small compartment, before sliding under the covers of the wide, comfortable bunk. Normally she read for a while before composing herself for sleep, but tonight the printed page failed utterly to hold her attention, and with a sigh she let the book drop and switched off the lamp.

But still she couldn't rest. The sheltering darkness, the glimmer of the stars beyond the porthole, the faint restful motion of the boat at anchor seemed unable to work their usual soothing magic for her, and she twisted and turned, pushing irritably in turn at the pillows, and the covering sheet, as if she suddenly found their presence constricting and intolerable.

Eventually she made herself lie immobile, forcing her lids to close over her aching eyes. If she deliberately emptied her mind, then surely some kind of peace would come.

What came instead was Nick's image, emblazoned on her mind, burning in her consciousness. Memories seemed to control her, like some relentless emotional treadmill, forcing her to relive every moment she had spent with him over the last month. In her mind, she heard every word, saw every look and gesture, rehearsed every tiny unimportant incident.

The stateroom seemed airless suddenly, her body on fire, in spite of the flimsiness of its covering. Her dry lips were moving, silently repeating his name over and over again, as a soundless crescendo of yearning built up inside her.

At first, his voice saying quietly, 'Alison, are you asleep?' seemed no more than another figment of her overwrought imagination. But the softly determined rap on the door which accompanied it was real enough, jerking her back to a full and startled consciousness. She sat up, clutching the sheet against her in an instinctively protective movement, as she stared across the stateroom at the locked door.

There was another knock at the door, and he spoke again, this time with faint impatience. 'Alison?'

Her hand stole up and covered her lips, as she watched the handle of the door turn quietly. When the door failed to yield, there was a pause, then the handle turned in the other direction, only to be released with an angrily frustrated rattle.

Not daring to move, ears straining, Alison heard Nick swear softly, then move away. With a little gasp of relief she turned on to her stomach, burying her face in the pillow, her heartbeat slow and unsteady. The impulse which had led her to lock her door had been well founded, it now seemed.

And the indications were that she had been over-optimistic in assuming Nick would not have noticed her state of emotional confusion. He was too experienced, his sexual perceptions far too highly tuned to leave him unaware of that sudden, disastrous urgency which had possessed her, and she had been a fool to suppose anything differently.

Certainly, he had never come near her stateroom before. Not until tonight, when he had recognised the unspoken needs in her and decided to capitalise on them, she thought bitterly. Well, thank heavens for the instinct which had prompted her to take her own precautions!

But even as she ruefully congratulated herself on her foresight, the lock rattled again, briefly and decisively, and as Alison propped herself up on her elbow in stunned disbelief, the door swung open and Nick walked in. He kicked the door shut behind him and walked over to the side of the bunk, his brows lifting sardonically as he looked down at her.

'No,' he observed mockingly, 'I didn't think you were asleep, in spite of all that determined silence.'

She found her voice. 'How did you get in here?'

'The master key,' he said. 'Something you overlooked, in your sudden passion for privacy.'

'It's not particularly sudden,' Alison said stonily. 'And up until now it's been respected. Will you please go, and leave me alone?'

He hunched a shoulder negligently. 'After we've talked, perhaps.'

'Wouldn't the morning be a more appropriate time for conversation?'

He smiled. 'It is morning, as it happens.'

'Daylight, then, if we're playing games with words,' Alison said shortly, plucking at the edge of the concealing sheet with restless fingers.

'We're not playing games at all.' Nick seated himself on the edge of the bunk. 'I came here to discuss a serious matter with you—a matter of business.'

Alison wetted her lips nervously with the tip of her tongue. 'Can't it wait? I'm tired now. I can't think straight at this time of night.'

'You don't need to think too hard.' His voice sounded cool and level. 'I came to ask if you would consider—amending the terms of our contract.'

The breath seemed to stop short in her lungs. She couldn't look at him. Instead she stared down, as if mesmerised, at the hem-stitched edge of the sheet. She began, 'I don't think I understand——'

'And I think you do,' Nick said quietly. 'When we made our bargain, we were strangers. I feel that's no longer the case. There's no reason why we shouldn't—re-think the situation.'

Alison found her voice from somewhere. 'We had an agreement . . .'

'Indeed we had,' he said drily. 'But circumstances—change. And so, for God's sake, can minds. We're not obliged to restrict our relationship, after all.'

'Unless we wish,' she said quickly. 'And I don't want to change everything. You said you'd leave me alone—you promised.'

He shrugged again. 'You made all kinds of promises too, darling, in church in front of witnesses. I'm sure I don't have to remind you what they were. The words may be old-fashioned, but they were singularly telling, all the same. All to do with loving and honouring and obeying.'

Her small breasts rose and fell under the rapid, shallow rush of her breathing. 'Is that what you want? My—obedience?'

'Not particularly.' His tone held a kind of wry impatience. 'Especially if it can be roughly translated as passive submission and resentment.

But it need not be like that, and I think you know it.' He put out a hand and cupped her slender neck, sliding his thumb along the delicate line of her collarbone. His voice softened. 'Alison, if you'd let me, I think I could make you happy.'

Her teeth ground into the soft flesh inside her lower lip. 'I'm happy already, thank you. I have everything I want—my home, and security for my family. I don't need anything else.'

There was a silence, then he said, 'And are your needs the only ones to be considered in all this?'

'Why, what's the matter?' she asked bitterly. 'Is even a month's celibacy too much for you to take?' She couldn't resist the jibe, but as soon as it was uttered she regretted it.

The caressing fingers stilled suddenly, and even in the shadowy light she could see the hardening of his face, the swift curl of his firm mouth. 'Congratulations, sweetheart,' he drawled. 'How clever of you to guess! So—are you going to—assuage my desires, like a dutiful wife should?'

She muttered between her teeth, 'I'll see you in hell first!'

Nick's laugh was soft, but without amusement. 'Harsh words, darling, which I'm tempted to make you eat.' His hand clamped at the back of her neck, compelling her forward to meet him as he bent towards her.

She began imploringly, 'Please—no . . .' then all further protests were stifled under the bruising fierceness of his mouth on hers.

She'd provoked him and she knew it, so she could not blame him for the suppressed anger which was dictating his treatment of her, although it could not prevent the ache in her heart at his lack of tenderness. And yet, in its way, as she dimly realised, that could be her salvation too. Because it fired her will to resist, as a gentler wooing would never have done.

Nick was lowering her back against her pillows, following her down, muttering something hoarse and hurried in his throat as he did so. The warm weight of his body against hers was an agonising enticement that she had to fight at all costs. Deliberately, she relaxed, letting her body go limp in his arms, as if signalling her submission.

Slowly Nick lifted his head, the blue eyes glittering down at her. He said huskily, 'Why the hell do you make me lose my temper? Darling, let me show you how it should be between us . . .'

Alison lay very still, her eyes fixed on his intent face, her swollen mouth trembling into a faint smile. Then she lifted her hands, sliding them inside the neckline of his robe, hearing the catch of his breath as her fingers moved tentatively on his hair-roughened skin. For a brief moment she let herself savour the forbidden pleasure of learning him through her fingertips, then she tensed, the slim hands becoming claws, raking and scratching at his bare chest.

He swore involuntarily, pulling himself upright away from the sudden savagery of her nails. He clicked on the lamp, and Alison winced, closing her eyes partly because of the sudden dazzle of the light, but more to hide from the sight of the long angry weals she had raised on his skin. She thought she might even have drawn blood, and shrank inwardly, wondering what kind of retribution she had invited in turn.

'You little bitch,' he said evenly, at last. 'What the hell was all that about?'

She made herself open her eyes and meet the cold anger of his gaze.

Her voice faltered a little. 'I'm—sorry. There are some tissues on the fitment . . .'

'I'm sure you're not sorry in the slightest.' Nick got to his feet, tightening the sash of his robe. 'So spare me the solicitude. And if by any chance you were hoping I'd die of blood poisoning, then forget it. We all heal quickly in our family, even from blows to the ego.' He paused. 'Under that demure exterior, you're pure hellcat, aren't you, Mrs Bristow?'

Alison knew an overwhelming desire to burst into tears. Instead, she said stonily, 'I never guaranteed anything different. Perhaps you should learn to take no for an answer.'

His contemptuous smile scorched her. 'Well, have no further worries on that score,' he said too pleasantly. 'You've made your point. I don't intend to ask that particular question again.' He walked to the door, and paused to fling her one last glance, as she crouched white-faced against her pillows. 'Sleep well, darling. And dream about your sterile little contract. I hope it keeps you warm at nights!'

The door slammed behind him.

Alison put out a shaking hand and plunged the stateroom into darkness again.

She lay still, waiting for the deep trembling inside her to subside.

She'd won, she supposed drearily, a kind of victory. So why then did she feel as if she'd suffered a major defeat?

CHAPTER SIX

As Alison emerged from the needlework shop she heard the first rumble of thunder, and she glanced up, grimacing at the inky clouds which were gathering. It had been a fine afternoon when she had set off into town, but her numerous errands, including a visit to the hairdresser, had all taken more time than she'd bargained for, and she was now running late. And likely to get wet too, she thought ruefully, cursing herself silently for not having brought an umbrella or even a headscarf with her.

For a moment she toyed with the idea of making a dive straight back to her car where it waited in the parking area at the far end of the High Street. Perhaps she could just outrun the storm. After all, there were only her mother's library books left to change, and they could surely wait for another day, she tried to persuade herself. As it was, most of her time had been taken up with her mother's 'one or two little things, darling' already. There'd been the foam pillow to replace the feather one, to which Mrs Mortimer had decided she might be allergic; there'd been the tapestry wool to match in a shade long since discontinued; the list of aspirin and throat pastilles from the chemist, and, finally, the library books, the choice of which would take longer than anything else.

She gave a faint groan and turned reluctantly towards the library. She would have to make time, that was all.

Only her mother, she thought bleakly, as she

ascended the shallow flight of stone steps towards the library, could expect her to spend the afternoon prior to the first major dinner party at Ladymead since her marriage in fulfilling an endless number of trivial tasks.

She should be at home now, supervising all the final details, and even making a few moments in which to relax and prepare herself mentally for what was bound to be something of an ordeal. It was the first time she would be on show as Nick's wife, playing her part as mistress of the house in front of the new managing director of Mortimers and several members of the board, and three of the executives from Nick's own company with their wives and girl-friends. She'd met none of them before, and it was inevitable that, at the beginning of the evening at least, she was going to be the cynosure of all eyes.

That was one of the reasons she had been to the hairdresser, to have her hair styled and blown into a new and infinitely more sophisticated flick-up coiffure. The girl whose deft fingers had created the transformation with scissors and mousse and hot-brush had been enthusiastic, and Alison had rather shyly shared her pleasure as she studied herself. She had had a manicure too, her nails tipped in a soft glowing shade of ruby which matched the new taffeta dress waiting in her bedroom back at Ladymead.

She had all the outer trappings, she thought, as she wandered round the bookshelves, looking for the ladylike detective stories which her mother preferred. All she needed to do now was feel like Mrs Nicholas Bristow, and that was easier said than done.

It was three weeks since they had returned from

their honeymoon, during which time she had seen little of Nick. He had brought her to Ladymead, satisfied himself that the alterations and decorations had been carried out precisely according to his instructions, been pleasant to her mother, and departed. Since then, he had returned twice, on each occasion staying overnight only, and even then, contact between them had been minimal. When others were present he was civil, she supposed, but little more.

In the few moments of privacy they had had together, he had made it very clear that their relationship was to be no more than that of employer and employee. He had laid down the ground rules for the way in which he wanted the house run in a coolly autocratic way that left no room for dissent, even if Alison had felt like offering it. As it was she had agreed quietly, almost numbly, to everything he had to say. And the list of people invited to tonight's dinner party, together with the instructions for the menu to be served, had reached her via a written memo from his office.

She wondered rather drearily what his secretary would have made of that. Not that it mattered. The woman, if she had worked for Nick for any length of time, would surely suspect the truth that Nick's unexpected marriage was nothing more than a put-up job. If the truth were known, she was probably already sending flowers to another lady, and booking intimate dinners at quiet restaurants.

Alison slammed the books she had chosen down on the counter, making the librarian jump slightly.

She had half expected when they flew back from Rhodes that they would spend the night in

London at Nick's house, but he had not even suggested such a thing. Clearly his London *pied-à-terre* was forbidden ground as far as she was concerned, part of his life that he intended to keep private. Until the newspapers got hold of it, she thought wretchedly as she pushed through the swing doors. Already, for all she knew, there might be stories in the tabloids about Nick and his newest conquest. She supposed she would know when people started giving her pitying glances.

She had been glancing through an English newspaper at Rhodes airport before their flight was called, and, almost like an omen, the first story she had read had revealed that, while they had been away, Hester Monclair's father-in-law had died, and her husband had inherited the baronetcy, making her now Lady Monclair.

Nick had seen the paper too. There was no way he could have missed the story, she had thought, stealing a sideways look at his harshly enigmatic face, the cold chiselled line of his mouth, but she could only guess at his reaction.

And it certainly wasn't anything she could introduce casually as a topic of conversation.

She paused on the library steps with an exclamation of dismay. While she'd been inside, the rain had arrived with a vengeance. Alison moved back into the shelter of the porch, glancing worriedly at her watch as she did so. She should have been back at Ladymead over half an hour ago. It wasn't that she didn't trust the staff to follow her instructions, but Nick, she knew, was expecting nothing short of perfection, and she would have liked to be able to take a long serene look round her domain and assure herself that he would have nothing to criticise.

That, after all, was the price he was demanding in return for her family's security, and honour demanded that she should pay it in full. But it wasn't easy to fulfil all her new responsibilities, and be at her mother's beck and call too.

She shivered slightly in her thin jacket, staring at the spearing raindrops with resentful eyes.

She had suggested, quite gently, that Catherine might enjoy the occasional trip into town herself, combining a shopping expedition with a rendez-vous for coffee or afternoon tea with some of her friends at one of the local cafés.

But her mother had stared at her with affronted, tragic eyes. 'I'm not strong enough to face anyone yet,' she had insisted. 'Marriage has changed you, Alison,' she had added. 'You never used to be so insensitive.'

Alison bit her lip. She had confided to Aunt Beth that she was worried that her mother might be becoming reclusive as a psychological result of her husband's death, but her aunt had given her an old-fashioned look, and a brief snort of derision.

'Psychological nonsense, my dear! Your mother is merely indulging her penchant for laziness, and you know it. She's far too comfortable in that suite of hers, being waited on hand and foot. You should prise her out of it, before she becomes totally entrenched. What does Nicholas think about it?'

Alison had murmured something evasive. Whatever her aunt and uncle might think about her hasty marriage, she couldn't even hint that the relationship between Nick and herself had already reached a stage where it was impossible to discuss anything of a personal nature. Her mother was her problem, and she would have to deal with her.

She looked at her watch again, and groaned silently. She couldn't hang about any longer, waiting for the rain to ease. She would have to make a dash for the car, she thought, putting a protective hand to her newly styled hair. Thanking heaven for her low-heeled shoes, she began to run along the soaking pavements. She was breathless when she reached the car, her tights splashed, and her hair hanging in rats' tails round her face. She surveyed herself defeatedly in the driving mirror as she pushed her key into the ignition. The engine whined sullenly and died.

She exclaimed aloud, 'Oh, no!' and tried again, forcing herself to move calmly and deliberately. Her car wasn't usually temperamental, but it didn't like damp weather. Once before, after a heavy rainstorm, it had refused to start for her. She thumped the dashboard in frustration, and jumped slightly as an echoing tap sounded on her window. She turned to see Simon Thwaite looking at her.

'Having trouble?' he asked, as she wound the window down.

'It seems so.' She forced a smile. 'Why do these things always happen when I'm in a tearing hurry? I think there's a spray you can use in this kind of emergency, but of course I don't have one with me.' She gave him an appealing look. 'I don't suppose you . . .?'

'I'm afraid not,' he said ruefully. 'The best I can offer is a lift home, if that will help.'

She sighed with relief. 'It would help enormously, Simon.'

'What will you do about your car?' He led the way across to his own BMW.

She shrugged. 'It will be safe enough where it is.

I'll ask the garage to take a look at it tomorrow. At the moment it's the least of my problems.'

'Oh.' He stared straight ahead of him through the windscreen. 'I thought you'd still be too bemused by newly-wedded bliss to have any problems.'

There was an edge to his voice, and Alison shifted uncomfortably in her seat. It was the first time she had encountered Simon since her marriage, and her gratitude for his offer of help had made her forget momentarily the awkwardness which had ensued when she had put in her notice at work and told him she was going to marry Nicholas Bristow.

She had no idea whether Simon had ever really entertained any serious intentions towards her himself, but it was clear her announcement had been a blow to his masculine pride if nothing else, and he had reacted with covert hostility, casting a cloud over her final days at the office.

She said lightly, 'I have a houseful of guests about to descend, and I'm running late, that's all. Not really so dire.'

'No.' He was silent for a moment, then he said, 'You're looking very well, Ally. Your tan suits you.'

'I think what's left of it is turning to rust,' she said drily. 'How's the property market?'

'Moving again. By the way, the Andersons are buying Stanton Grange, just as you predicted.'

Alison gave a gurgle of laughter. 'I knew she couldn't resist that jacuzzi! She kept going back to have another peep at it.'

'Yes.' He paused again. 'I haven't found a replacement for you yet, Alison. We miss you at the office, and that's a fact. I suppose you wouldn't consider coming back?'

She was genuinely taken aback. It was the last thing she had expected.

She said slowly, 'I'd have to give that some thought, Simon. And discuss it with Nick, of course,' she added.

'Take all the time you need,' said Simon, overtaking a van. 'It occurred to me that as your husband's so obviously a busy man, you might find yourself with a lot of leisure on your hands.'

Alison sat very still. So Nick's infrequent appearances had already been noted and discussed, she thought wretchedly. Well, what else could she expect in such a small community?

She shrugged, hoping for nonchalance. 'I'm not really a lady of leisure, you know. And I know Nick has plans to do a lot of entertaining in the coming weeks. I could have my hands full.'

'Well, as I say, think about it,' he said pleasantly. For the remainder of the journey they talked on safe neutral topics like the changeable weather, and the new production being planned by the local operatic society.

The kind of things they'd always talked about, Alison thought, which perhaps explained why being with Simon had never filled her with the kind of unnamed longings that simply hearing Nick's voice on the phone could inspire.

Not that she was proud of that, she assured herself flatly. In fact, she was deeply, hotly ashamed of her own weakness. Life would have been so much easier, so much more acceptable if she'd married someone like Simon. He might never have set her on fire, but she would not have experienced this agonising, gnawing emptiness either.

Arrived back at Ladymead, she thanked him

rather stiltedly for his help, promised she would be in touch, and paused at the door to wave politely and smile as he drove away. Then with a small sigh, she turned and walked into the house.

'Where have you been?' Nick's sharp question fell across her consciousness like a whiplash, and she started visibly as she looked up and saw him coming downstairs towards her.

'Oh,' she said lamely, her heart sinking. 'You're—back.'

'Naturally,' he returned grimly. 'We do have guests this evening, in case you'd forgotten,' he added bitingly.

'Of course I haven't forgotten. Everything's ready for them.' Or she hoped it was, she thought, surreptitiously crossing her fingers in the folds of her skirt.

His lip curled. 'Does that include yourself?'

For the moment, she'd forgotten her ruined hair. She touched it nervously. 'I—I got caught in the storm, I'm afraid.'

'So I see,' he said coldly. 'Don't you ever listen to weather forecasts? Or was your reason for going into town so overwhelming that it couldn't be put off?'

She could hardly say she'd been to the hairdresser, looking as she did. She bit her lip. 'I had one or two things to do—shopping and so on.'

'Does the "so on" include disposing of your car?' he demanded. 'You certainly didn't return in it.'

Alison sighed. 'It's still in the High Street car park. The rain must have got into the electrics, because it wouldn't start. It's happened before.'

'Has it really? Then I shall take steps to ensure it doesn't happen again.' He walked across the hall and went into the dining room. Alison set down her shopping and went after him. He was standing staring critically at the table.

'I hope you like the lace mats. They're rather old,' she said, hurrying her words a little. 'And I did the flowers myself.'

She sounded like a child waiting for a word of praise, she thought with self-derision.

'You—you did say you'd see to the wines,' she pounded on into the silence.

'Yes, I did.' Nick gave a faint nod. 'Everything seems satisfactory. I presume there was no difficulty with Mrs Horner over waiting at table?'

'Oh, no, she's quite used to it.' She hesitated. 'But if it's going to be a regular occurrence, I might need alternative help.'

'Then you'd better find it.' He moved to the door. 'I suppose you've checked the drawing room?'

'Hardly,' she protested. 'I've only just got back.'

'I'm aware of that,' he said icily. 'Perhaps it's time you gave some thought to your priorities. Understand this, Alison, I expect your duties here to take precedence over—gallivanting into town to meet your friends.'

'But I didn't!' she protested, stung by the injustice of it.

His brows rose. 'You hardly came back by taxi,' he uttered flatly.

Of course, she thought, his room was at the front of the house, and he had seen her arrive with Simon.

She said, 'That was a coincidence. Simon just happened to be there when I was trying to start the car.'

'Very convenient,' Nick drawled. 'But I really

think I shall have to supply you with a more reliable vehicle, my sweet. I can't have my wife stranded in car parks, dependent on passing knights errant. Especially when the experience leaves her looking so dishevelled,' he added sarcastically. 'Perhaps you'd like to go and make yourself presentable—after you've fulfilled your duties down here, of course.'

Alison drew a deep breath of disbelief, then lifted her hand in a parody of a salute. 'Yes—sir,' she said. 'Will that be all, sir?'

His eyes narrowed. 'Provoke me again, Alison, and it will be far from all. You may not be prepared to be my wife, but you'll damned well give your undivided attention to being my housekeeper. Is that clearly understood?'

She said dully, 'Perfectly. In future, I'll do my best to live up to your rather exacting standards.'

She gave the drawing room a brief formal inspection, then went upstairs to her mother's suite.

Mrs Mortimer greeted her with a trace of fretfulness. 'What a time you've been, darling! I thought I heard the car ages ago. Did you get my wool? I've been waiting for it.'

An irritable reply hovered on Alison's lips. Her mother's tapestry work proceeded by fits and starts, and always had, neglected sometimes for weeks on end. But she controlled herself. 'I did the best I could,' she returned temperately. 'Mrs Marsden at the shop suggested it might be better in future to buy enough of each shade to complete the design.'

Mrs Mortimer sniffed. 'Well, of course, she would say so. In that way she sells more wool. I usually have skeins left over. And did they have the new Mary Cornell at the library?'

'I'm afraid not. In fact, there's a waiting list for it, so I put your name down. They'll send a card when it's available.'

Her mother's mouth tightened. 'A waiting list!' she commented rather shrilly. 'Things have certainly changed! In Mrs Harris's day, new books were always put on one side for me.'

'Which was hardly fair to the other borrowers,' Alison pointed out drily. 'I brought you these instead.'

Mrs Mortimer pursed her lips discontentedly. 'I suppose they'll have to do,' she said grudgingly. 'I don't care for Ellen Smart any more—her last two were far too Americanised.' She put the books to one side. 'And did you think of the peppermint creams?'

Alison's head was beginning to ache. 'Peppermint creams? But you never mentioned . . .'

'But you know I always have a box of the special Hargraves ones at the weekend,' Mrs Mortimer said crossly. 'You really are getting rather thoughtless, darling! Surely I don't have to think of everything for myself?'

'It might be better if you did,' Alison countered wearily. 'Then I might have more time to spend on my responsibilities here.'

'I should think you could manage that with one hand tied behind your back,' Mrs Mortimer said acidly. 'It's hardly new to you, after all. When your poor father was alive, you coped perfectly well.'

'I coped, certainly,' Alison agreed. 'But things are very different now.'

'They seem to be, indeed.' Mrs Mortimer's hand went up and fiddled with her pearls. 'Did I hear Nicholas return some time ago?'

'Probably,' Alison said evenly. 'Did you want to speak to him about something?'

'Oh, no,' Mrs Mortimer disclaimed hurriedly. 'It's just that—we seem to see so little of him.' She gave Alison a sharp look. 'I hope he's not neglecting you.'

'On the contrary,' Alison returned ironically, 'he couldn't be more attentive.'

It had amazed and infuriated her on her return from the honeymoon to discover that her mother had apparently decided to totally disregard the real reasons for the marriage, and behave as if Nicholas was her ideal choice as a son-in-law.

Now Mrs Mortimer lifted a restive shoulder. 'Well, if you say so, darling.' She shook her head. 'Although there are times when it's small wonder to me that he does stay away so much. Have you seen yourself lately? You look like something the cat dragged in. I thought you were going to have your hair done for the party this evening.'

'It must have slipped my mind,' Alison said tiredly. 'If you'll excuse me now, I'll go and start on the salvage job.'

'I think you should.' Her mother nodded her affirmation as she reached for the pile of library books. 'After all, darling, if you let yourself go like this, you can hardly hope to hold the attention of an attractive man like Nicholas.'

'Then it's fortunate I have no such expectation,' Alison said more sharply than she intended. She saw an affronted expression cross her mother's face, and sighed inwardly. 'I'm sorry, Mother—I suppose I'm a little het up about tonight. Will you come down about half past seven?'

'Of course,' Mrs Mortimer said rather coldly. 'I

must say, Alison, I hoped marriage would cure you of this ridiculous shyness, but it seems, if anything, to be worse. Do put some colour on your face, dear. You look like a ghost!'

The ghost of something the cat dragged in, Alison thought, as she made her way to her bedroom, and didn't know whether to giggle or burst into tears.

She had hung her new dress on the outside of the fitted wardrobe before she went out, but the sight of it gave her no pleasure, rather serving to fuel her simmering resentment. It was far too glamorous for a mere housekeeper, she thought bitterly, ramming it back on the rail among the other dresses. She would wear something more suited to her station, she decided stormily, scanning along the hanging rail, and she knew precisely what, as well.

It had been an attempt at 'the little black dress' which her mother had always claimed was an indispensable adjunct of every woman's wardrobe, only it had never quite worked. Alison had bought it in a hurry, thinking it might do, but it never had. Its severe lines did nothing for her slenderness, and she had always felt swamped and dowdy in it. As she pulled the dress off its hanger, she became aware of something else, beneath it on the floor of the wardrobe. A box . . .

Of course, she thought, impatient with herself; it was the box of exquisite undies Aunt Beth had given her. She took off the lid and studied the contents, frowning a little. They were so beautiful, it seemed criminal to leave them shut away like this, unworn. She extracted a set of diaphanous ivory silk cami-knickers and the suspender belt that matched them, and took them into the bathroom, while she showered and washed her hair. She would try them on, she thought, although she wasn't altogether convinced that she would wear them. Yet once she had felt the silky, seductive glide of them on her skin, she was lost.

Sitting at her dressing table, applying the hand-dryer to her damp hair, she could hardly believe the image she saw in the mirror. When her hair was dry, she brushed it straight back from her face and anchored it with pins in a prim bun at the nape of her neck. The contrast between the demureness of her hairstyle and the cloudy sensuality of her attire could not have been more complete, she thought, her mouth twisting slightly. It was almost—erotic.

An impression dispelled the moment she put on the black dress. In the few second it took to fasten the zip, she was transformed from embryo seductress into dull nonentity. She sighed a little. Well, maybe it was safer that way.

She could hear her mother's silvery tones coming from the drawing room when she got downstairs. She hesitated, then vanished to the kitchen, to make sure that Cook, and her niece who helped her on hectic occasions, hadn't encountered any unexpected snags. But everything was going smoothly.

'As you should know, Miss Alison,' Cook told her placidly. 'And your place is in the drawing room, not here, where you might get something spilled on your dress,' she added, with a dubious look at the garment in question.

'Oh, don't scold me,' Alison appealed mischievously. 'I just want to relax for a few moments before the fray, that's all.'

'Well, you're in the way here,' Cook told her

severely. 'And Mr Bristow will be wondering where you are. And leave those canapés alone!' she added in a voice of doom. 'Why, Miss Alison, for all you're grown up and married, you're like a naughty child sometimes, I swear you are!'

'But anchovies have always been my weakness, you know that,' Alison said plaintively. She was in no hurry to go the drawing room. She wanted no awkward questions about the black dress until it was too late for her to change.

'And other people will like them too, I daresay. Now leave them, there's a love. And isn't that the doorbell? Your guests are arriving, and you're not there to receive them.'

Alison laughed, and slid off the kitchen table. 'I'm on my way!'

She reached the drawing room while the first arrivals were still dispensing with their coats and wraps, but her lateness had been noticed. And laughter gurgled within her, as she saw how Nick's initial glare of annoyance changed dramatically to sheer incredulity as he assimilated her appearance. She returned his searching stare with a defiant lift of her chin, although she was quaking inwardly, then, as he started towards her, his brows drawn thunderously together, he turned, smiling with calm warmth to meet the new chairman of Mortimers as Mrs Horner showed him and his wife into the room.

The next few minutes was totally taken up with new arrivals and introductions, and the handing round of drinks and canapés, so there was no chance of Nick saying anything privately to her, although it was obvious, by the fulminating glances he occasionally bestowed on her, that he was anxious to do so.

And as she shook hands and murmured conventional greetings to a succession of chic, well-groomed and bejewelled women, Alison found herself wishing she had not allowed her resentment to get the better of her. They were all too pleasant, and generally, she thought, too kind to let their feelings show, but she could sense the shock in them as they were introduced. They must all be wondering why the sexy, dynamic Nicholas Bristow had saddled himself with a plain, dowdy freak as a wife. And she wasn't sure she could blame them.

She had intended to annoy Nicholas, but even though she had succeeded, probably beyond her wildest dreams, she had done herself no credit either.

In fact, the whole day had been something of a nightmare, and when Mrs Horner came to announce dinner, Alison would not have been in the least surprised if she had told them the kitchen had exploded, and the food was ruined.

She saw her guests seated, then took her own place at the foot of the long table, opposite Nicholas but far enough away from him to be safe, at least for the moment.

She gave her attention to the people sitting near her, responding to their appreciative comments as the bowls of chilled avocado soup with the swirls of cream were placed in front of them. The meal was beginning, and she could relax.

Then she looked up and found Nicholas watching her, his blue eyes skimming her like an Arctic breeze, and she shivered involuntarily. Because eventually, however delicious the meal, however warm the hospitality and interesting the conversation, all these strangers would leave.

And sooner or later she would have to face the reckoning with Nicholas.

CHAPTER SEVEN

'MARVELLOUS party! Thank you so much.' 'We have enjoyed ourselves.' The words of thanks and parting reverberated in Alison's head as she went into her bedroom and closed the door behind her, a stifled sigh of relief escaping her lips as she leaned against its solid panels.

Outwardly, the evening had indeed been a great success, the meal a triumph, the after-dinner conversation in the drawing room so interesting, that everyone was clearly loth to tear themselves away.

But, for Alison, the evening had been a personal nightmare. Whatever had possessed her to do such a crazy thing? she asked herself wretchedly, chewing at the soft inner flesh of her lower lip. Oh, yes, she'd made a fool of Nicholas, which was what she had intended, but she had made an even bigger fool of herself. And the knowledge of the stupidity of her own conduct had exacerbated her natural shyness, so that their guests not only must think she was a frump, but a tongue-tied idiot as well, she thought miserably.

Nick had accompanied Ian Farnham, his second-in-command, out to his car for a final word, and Alison had seized the opportunity to escape.

She had made the excuse to her mother that she had a headache—which, in a way, was no more than the truth. Her scalp felt tender as a result of wearing her hair wrenched back all evening, and

every pin she had used to secure the unbecoming
bun seemed to be burrowing into her head. She
removed them carefully, then shook her ill-used
hair loose, as she walked over to her dressing table
and sank down on the stool. God, but she looked
awful! Pale, washed-out, because she'd used no
make-up but a smudge of lipstick, and drowned in
that monster of a dress. She groaned and picked
up her hairbrush, stroking it gently through her
hair, restoring it to its usual shining order.

Well, she thought, at least she had managed to
postpone the inevitable confrontation with
Nicholas, even though she couldn't put it off for ever.

But even that forlorn sense of reassurance went
by the board, as her bedroom door opened
forcefully and Nick strode in. He closed the door
with a swift, backward kick of one well-shod foot,
then stood, hands on hips, regarding her grimly.

Alison swallowed, then turned slowly to face
him, forcing herself to a semblance of composure.

She said with a certain hauteur, 'Didn't my
mother explain . . .?

'That you have a headache?' Nicholas supplied.
'Yes, she mentioned it. And I'm here to tell you,
sweetheart, that if you play me any more tricks
like tonight's, you're going to ache in a very
different part of your anatomy!'

'I don't understand what you mean,' she said
defiantly. 'I—I thought it went very well.'

'You understand perfectly well,' drawled Nick.
'So—where did you get the dress? A jumble sale?
What a pity you couldn't find one that actually
fitted!'

Alison felt the betraying colour seep into her
face, but she kept going just the same. 'I'm sorry if
you don't care for my taste in clothes.'

His mouth curled. 'I'd be sorry too if I thought for one moment this was a genuine sample of it. No, darling. Your decision to appear in front of our guests looking like something out of a third-rate touring production of *Rebecca* was quite deliberate, and we both know it.'

'I know nothing of the kind,' Alison said stiffly. 'And I think you're being very insulting. I'd be glad if you'd go now, and leave me in peace.'

'I'm sure you would,' he said derisively. 'But I haven't finished with you yet. I can appreciate why you might wish to ignore the jewellery I've given you. It's hardly in keeping with your image of Downtrodden Drudge, after all. But you could at least have worn your bloody engagement ring. Or have you left that somewhere too—like the car?'

Alison controlled a little gasp. The failure to wear his sapphire had been a complete oversight, not a deliberate affront, little though he might believe that now. A sense of guilt refuelled her rising temper.

'And why should I wear it?' she demanded scornfully. 'To demonstrate to everyone how generous you are—and how rich? I'm sure they know that already. I never wanted an engagement ring from you, Nick. I was never your fiancée, just as I'm not your wife. The truth is I'm just the housekeeper. I know it, and you know it, so why shouldn't the rest of the world be aware of it too? And now get out of my room!'

He said softly, 'This is my room, darling. It belongs to me, along with most of the other things in this bloody house—yourself included. And if you don't care for your role—self-imposed, I might remind you—then that can be remedied, right now.'

He walked towards her, stalking her like some predatory jungle animal, she thought, fear catching in her throat. She jumped up, knocking over her dressing stool.

'I asked you to go.' Her voice sounded young and breathless.

'I heard you,' Nick said coolly. 'But I'm staying—at least long enough to ensure that you'll never wear that damned dress again!'

She backed away. 'Please—leave me alone. I'll throw the dress away—I promise I will.'

'You'll have to.' He was still advancing on her, and Alison found herself, literally, with her back to the wall, and nowhere left to retreat to.

'No!' She put out her hands to ward him off, and his fingers clamped round her slender wrists, jerking her towards him.

'Experiencing a few regrets?' he asked with a low laugh. 'Well, you started this, my sweet. Just remember that.' He swung her round, and she felt his hands at the back of her dress, where the cowled neckline dipped towards the zip-fastening. She began to struggle, trying to drag herself away from him.

'Don't! I—I'll take it off—really . . .'

'And deprive me of the pleasure?' Nick drawled. He didn't bother with the zip. His strong hands gripped the material wrenching at it, until it gave with a tearing sound that echoed in her head like a scream.

As it began to slip off her shoulders, she tried to grab at it, but Nick forestalled her, using his superior strength to drag the crumpled and ripped fabric downwards to fall in a dark mass at her feet. His arm was like a band of steel round her waist as he lifted her clear of the tangling folds.

'Put me down!' Nearly crying with humiliation, Alison kicked out at him.

He obeyed so promptly that she almost fell over.

She turned to face him, like some small creature at bay, words of wild indignation trembling incoherently on her lips. But never to be uttered.

Because suddenly she saw him looking at her—and remembered too late exactly what she'd been wearing under all that ugly black.

He was totally arrested, his eyes travelling over her in incredulous absorption as he took in every provocative detail, from the heavy band of lace that outlined the thrust of her small breasts to the fragile suspenders which fastened her stockings.

Nick said, too quietly, 'You're full of surprises tonight, aren't you, my sweet? Are you leading some kind of secret life, or was all this glamour for your own eyes only—because, if so, it's an appalling waste.'

Alison was mute with embarrassment, hot with shame as she tried desperately to cover herself with her hands, knowing, as she did so, that it was already far too late.

Never taking his eyes from her, Nick bent and righted the fallen dressing stool, then shrugged off his dinner jacket, dropping it across the padded seat. He pulled his black tie loose and discarded that too, and, still in silence, began to unfasten his shirt.

She found a voice from somewhere. 'I want you to leave—now.'

His mouth twisted. 'I don't think you know what you want. You're two women, Mrs Bristow, do you know that? All prim, businesslike self-control on the outside, but underneath——' there was a disturbingly husky note in his voice, as he pulled off his shirt, 'a little sexy siren, just waiting to be discovered. You're not sending me away now, darling. I intend to explore these hidden depths of yours to the full.'

'You—you can't!' Shocked, Alison tried to rally her flagging defiance. 'I won't let you!'

He smiled rather cynically. 'I'm not seeking your permission.'

'You promised me.' She lifted her chin, her tone lashing him scornfully. 'You said you wouldn't ask again.'

'And I'm not asking either,' he said softly. 'This time I'm taking.'

'I should have known I couldn't trust you!' Alison tried to edge sideways. It had suddenly occurred to her that a swift, undignified scramble across that enormous bed would bring her almost within reach of the bathroom door, which could be bolted behind her. It wasn't much of a refuge, but she couldn't believe that Nick would risk alerting the entire household by kicking a door down to get to her. She moistened her lips with the tip of her tongue, trying unobtrusively to estimate the distance that divided her from her sanctuary.

He laughed. 'Then isn't it good to know that your low opinion of me is perfectly justified?' he mocked.

Alison drew a breath and dived sideways for the bed, trying to fling herself across its unruffled surface. But Nick was too quick for her. As she tried to roll sideways he was there too, his weight pinning her remorselessly to the yielding mattress.

'Such ardour!' he jeered softly. 'I would have carried you, darling, if you'd just waited another second.' With insulting ease, he pinioned both her wrists with one hand. 'Just in case you're tempted to try your wildcat tactics again,' he told her, smiling faintly down into her dilated eyes. 'I don't intend to spend my married life permanently scarred.'

'Then let me go.' She was reduced to begging now, but slowly, he shook his head.

'Not this time, Alison. As we've previously established, celibacy doesn't suit me.' He slid a finger under one fragile shoulder strap and then the other, drawing them gently down her slender arms. As he did so, the lace that covered her breasts began to slip down too, revealing their soft rose-tipped curves to the intensity of his gaze. His dark head bent, and gently his mouth caressed each taut nipple in turn, making her gasp out loud as she was transfixed by a shaft of heated, unwelcome pleasure. He said quietly, 'And I don't think it suits you either, my innocent wife,' murmuring the words against her warm flesh.

'Don't pretend you haven't found adequate consolation.' Alison's own voice sounded faintly slurred, even to her own ears. The seductive movement of his lips and tongue against her reluctant skin was making it difficult for her to think coherently, never mind speak.

He lifted his head and stared down at her, his face hardening, the dark flush along his cheekbones deepening perceptibly. Then he shrugged. 'Believe what you want,' he said curtly. He sat up, and for a moment she thought her jibe had secured a reprieve for her, but he had moved only to facilitate the removal of the rest of his clothes, she soon realised.

She closed her eyes tightly, blocking out the sight of him, trying desperately to find some way of armouring her vulnerable senses and emotions against this enforced possession.

She had thought simply becoming Nick's wife in name only as a high price to pay for Ladymead and the security of her family. Now, she realised, she had not known the half of it. Once she belonged to him, she would have no defences left, and no self-respect either. Wife or not, to Nick she would be just another conquest, a novelty because she had actually had the temerity to resist his previous advances.

His mouth brushed hers, softly and sensuously. 'Now it's your turn,' he whispered.

He unfastened her suspenders and rolled down her delicate stockings, his hands slow and infinitely careful, his mouth caressing every inch of her slender legs from her trembling thighs down to her arched insteps.

A little sigh was impelled from her, and her body twisted restlessly, seeking an appeasement she barely understood.

'Take it easy, sweetheart,' Nick muttered huskily. 'We have a hell of a way to go yet.'

He kissed her lips deeply and urgently, parting their softness so that he could explore her mouth's moist inner warmth. For a moment she was passive beneath the unaccustomed intimacy, then slowly, stiffly, as if they were acting of their own volition, her arms lifted and locked round his neck, and she returned the kiss, shyly at first, and then with shuddering pleasure, now that the exploration was mutual.

His hands were stroking her breasts, his long fingers teasing the aroused peaks, creating a torrid, shaking excitement in her innermost being. It was almost shaming to discover how swift and ready her responses were, but impossible to deny or conceal them.

His mouth left hers to imprint little kisses across her temples and cheekbones, brushing her hair aside to seek the whorls and crevices of her ears, and the sensitivity of her pulsating throat.

She felt the shiver of silk against her body in the gentlest of frictions as Nick's sure hands uncovered her completely. He raised himself slightly away from her, his eyes glittering as he took in every inch of her slender nakedness, his hand sweeping down her body from shoulder to thigh in a gesture of total ownership.

Her eyes were cloudy with desire, her breath sighing through passion-swollen lips as she looked back at him.

He drew a sharp, harsh breath, then his hand moved—sought her, found her with a devastating intimacy, his touch silk and fire as he caressed her, his fingers lingering, pressuring, luring her body to open to him and yield up its final secret.

His mouth possessed her breasts again with a new fierceness, a new demand, and she moaned in her throat, savouring a fresh, more urgent delight as his lips tugged at her tumescent nipples.

Her hands slid down the long length of his spine as she arched herself against his body, lifting her slender hips in silent surrender to his invasive strength.

'Dear God, you take my breath away!' The husky words seemed torn out of his throat, his hands continuing their expert, devilish, miraculous incitement of her.

She was reaching some crisis point; every instinct in her pleasure-racked body told her that. She could hear a voice, only just recognisable as her own, whispering, 'Oh, please—oh, please . . .' over and over again.

Nick groaned something in reply, then his body moved over hers in stark purpose.

At first there was pain, but the torment of needing to be one with him was greater, she discovered, as her inexperienced body unclenched to receive him. He was still for a long moment, gently brushing the tiny beads of sweat from her forehead with his lips, then kissing her eyes, and the tip of her small straight nose as he traced a sensuous path back to her lips.

Mouths locked, bodies locked, they began to move together. He was being gentle with her, she knew, but there was no need. The warmth of his body against hers, the heat of him inside her were triggering new and devastating responses. Digging her hands into his shoulders, she twined her legs round him in mute offering. At once, the rhythm of his possession deepened, intensified as he allowed full rein to his own needs.

And suddenly she was lost, submerged and drowning in a wild, sweet violence of sensation which transcended all other human experience. She cried out her joy against his kiss, and felt his lean, powerful body shudder in her arms.

The aftermath held a peace more complete than she had ever known. She rested in Nick's embrace, her mind floating, drifting in dreamlike contentment. When at last he moved, she uttered a small throaty protest, then relaxed again as she felt the bedcovers drawn over her. Nick slid down beside her, pulling her against him so that her head was pillowed on his chest. She turned her face into his body, relishing the warm scent of him, the firm texture of his skin, then, murmuring drowsily, she fell asleep.

*   *   *

Alison woke, as she always did, a few minutes before the harsh buzz of the alarm. She stretched out an arm to switch the buzzer off, then paused, her attention caught by an unfamiliar sound—the gushing of water, not too far away.

She frowned, propping herself up on one elbow as she listened. There was no mistaking it. It was the sound of the shower in her bathroom. She shook her head, pushing back her tumbled hair, then paused, her attention totally arrested as she saw the scatter of discarded clothing on the floor. The warm clouds of sleep still enveloping her brain were dispelled with a vengeance as the memory of what had happened the previous night flooded back to her. She collapsed back against her pillows, her heart banging crazily against her ribs, as every detail unfolded in her mind's eye, like some erotic action replay.

Oh God, she moaned silently, lifting her hands to her burning face. So all her pride, her fierce determination to keep Nick at arms' length at all costs had faltered and failed at the first challenge!

She closed her eyes, wishing that she wasn't blessed, or cursed, with such total recall. Then, perhaps, she might have forgotten those last dreaming moments in Nick's arms before sleep claimed her, and the way she had whispered, 'I love you' into his skin.

Of all the pathetic, humiliating confessions! Alison lashed herself, her small teeth digging viciously into her lower lip. Not content with losing a major battle, she had practically surrendered the war as well by revealing the pitiful extent of her obsession with him. Wasn't it enough that her body no longer held any secrets for him? she asked herself painfully. Had he really had to ravish her mind and emotions too? She felt exposed, vulnerable and frightened as she listened to the rush of water.

The forgotten alarm sounded stridently, and she jumped almost guiltily, harassed by another thought. In a few minutes Mrs Horner would be arriving with her morning tea, and the thought of her face, when confronted by the blatant evidence of what had taken place the previous night, galvanised Alison into sudden frenzied activity.

She snatched a pair of her usual practical pyjamas from a drawer and put them on, fumbling the buttons into their holes in her haste. If she'd only stuck to simple chain store undies instead of succumbing to the glamour of all that silk and lace, she might have less to regret this morning, she thought wretchedly, as she snatched up the clothes on the floor and bundled them out of sight into the nearest wardrobe.

'Tidying up?' Nick's approach had been silent across the thick pile of the carpet, and Alison started as his arms went round her, drawing her back against him. He smelled cool, damp and fresh and the prompting to relax into his embrace, turning willingly into his arms, was almost irresistible. Instead, she tensed, pushing at his hands.

'What's the matter?' he asked.

'Mrs Horner will be here at any moment with my tea,' she said flatly.

He shrugged negligently. 'That's all right. We'll send her back for another cup.'

Alison took a deep breath. 'But I'd prefer you not be found here—if you don't mind,' she added hurriedly, conscious that the muscles in the encircling arms had tautened.

'I think I do mind,' Nick said after a pause. 'I'm

your husband, and I think that entitles me to be here. And as Mrs Horner has been married herself for nearly thirty years, she's hardly likely to be shattered by the realisation that we've slept together.'

Alison felt colour heat her skin. 'Nevertheless,' she began, but he interrupted her, turning her inexorably to face him, and running a sensuous finger across her parted lips.

'Nevertheless, it would be better if you stopped arguing, and came back to bed with me,' he said softly. 'We have things to discuss.'

She gave him a mutinous look. 'We can talk like this just as well.'

The dark brows drew together slightly. 'You can, perhaps,' he said, 'muffled up to the ears in those weird garments, but I'm wearing nothing but a damp towel, and it's getting decidedly chilly.'

He picked her up bodily and carried her over to the bed, settling her back against the pillows before he unhitched the towel from round his hips and joined her.

Alison lay staring rigidly ahead of her. She hadn't been able to avert her gaze fast enough, and she was infuriated to find how swiftly her senses had been stirred by that brief, unavoidable glimpse of his naked body.

There was a silence, then Nick said drily, 'You look like a lady suffering from a severe case of regret.'

'You said you wanted to talk,' she reminded him stonily.

'So I did,' he agreed, still with that thoughtful crease between his brows. 'I have to go back to London today, Alison, and I want you to come with me.'

Sheer surprise rendered her dumb for a moment, and her eventual 'Why?' emerged as a strangled croak.

'Well,' he said softly, 'there's the matter of your new wardrobe to supervise.'

'The clothes I already have are perfectly adequate for my position here,' she said stiltedly.

'Ah!' Nick smiled wickedly, and she felt his hand move to stroke the curve of her hip under the sheltering covers. 'But perhaps I want to buy you something appropriate for some of the other positions I have in mind.'

Alison stiffened. 'Don't!'

'And what does that ban cover?' he asked evenly. 'Teasing you? Or touching you?'

'Both.' She flicked her dry mouth with the tip of her tongue. 'Nick, please go!'

'When I'm ready,' he said rather grimly. 'You seem very anxious to be rid of me. Last night . . .'

'Last night I behaved like an animal,' Alison said hurriedly. 'I don't particularly want to be reminded of it.'

'You behaved like a woman,' he said, after a glacial pause. 'And you should be proud of that, not ashamed, my little prude. My God, you were a revelation . . .'

'I suppose that's intended to be a compliment,' she said tautly. 'Forgive me if I'm not very grateful. And if I don't congratulate you on your expertise, which I'm sure is considerable.' She swallowed. 'Is that why you want me in London with you? To indulge in more sexual acrobatics?'

His face hardened. 'If that's how you wish to phrase it,' he drawled. 'You proved an apt pupil, my darling. You can hardly blame me for wanting to continue with your lessons.'

'I suppose I should be gratified that I have novelty value at least,' Alison said tonelessly. Inside, she was dissolving in wretchedness. 'But I'm afraid that isn't enough to tempt me to abandon my life here. That's what I married you for, after all, and not your prowess in bed, however celebrated.'

Nick was very still suddenly. He said softly, 'I see. And may I know what's so important here that everything else pales into insignificance beside it?'

She said woodenly, 'This is my home. As you reminded me yesterday, I have duties and responsibilities here—not least, to my mother.'

'Ah, yes,' Nick said silkily, 'your mother. I realise, of course, that she thoroughly enjoys very poor health, but it didn't occur to me she was using you as an unpaid messenger girl either. Yet I gather from various remarks she made during the course of the evening that most of those parcels you were festooned with yesterday were for her.'

'And what if they were?' Alison refused to meet his gaze. 'She—she isn't strong. And it's my pleasure to do things for her.'

'It doesn't seem to you that you have other duties and other—pleasures which might take priority over running errands for your mother?' His tone was deceptively light; there was anger simmering just below the surface, as Alison was quick to recognise. 'Does the fact that I want you with me really count for so little?'

She made herself shrug. 'That wasn't part of the bargain.' She paused. 'Besides, I have another reason for wanting to stay down here. As it happens, I've been offered my old job back.'

'I hope you turned it down.' The anger was overt now.

'I did nothing of the kind. I said I'd think about it.'

'Well, you can stop thinking right now. If you need a job, you have one here.'

'I did both before, and can again. After all, you're here so little, it can make very little difference to you.'

'That doesn't mean I want my wife to be at another man's beck and call,' Nick said tersely. 'Besides, has it occurred to you that your return to the world of real estate might be rather shortlived? Judging by your total inexperience, I doubt very much whether you took any precautions last night, and I sure as hell didn't. You could be pregnant.'

He sounded casual to the point of being callous, Alison thought, pain striking at her.

She shrugged again. 'Perhaps,' she said. 'But that doesn't mean I have to stay pregnant.'

'You little bitch,' he said slowly, the blue eyes harsh with contempt as they looked her over. 'If I thought you meant that, I'd handcuff you to my bloody wrist for the duration!'

'Such paternal feelings,' Alison said mockingly. 'Surely it can't be a totally unfamiliar situation for you?'

'The only unfamiliar situation,' Nick said softly, 'is my overwhelming desire to slap you hard. I think I'd better get out of here before I succumb to temptation.' Angrily, he thrust aside the covers and swung his long legs to the floor, kicking the discarded towel impatiently away from him as he did so. He gave Alison one last, fulminating glance, then stalked across the room to the communicating door between their rooms.

It slammed behind him, awaking reverberations which rang in Alison's head like a death knell. She lay curled into a ball, her clenched fist pressed against her mouth, listening to him move about, opening and shutting drawers and cupboards. Then she heard his own door thud shut, and his stride going past her room and down the corridor. Back to London. Away from her.

When her door opened she sat up, hope flooding her absurdly, only to be confronted by the homely figure of Mrs Horner.

'My, but Mr Bristow was in a hurry to be off,' she commented, setting down the tray, and drawing back the curtains. 'It's not much fun for him having to rush back to work after a party.' She pursed her lips as she looked at Alison. 'And you're looking pale, Miss Alison. Didn't you sleep well?'

'I had a nightmare,' said Alison, picking up her cup.

Mrs Horner tutted. 'Nasty things, but soon forgotten.'

Not this one, Alison thought when she was alone again. This particular nightmare of loneliness and heartache could haunt her for the rest of her life.

CHAPTER EIGHT

ALISON replaced the telephone receiver and looked across at the desk where Simon was working. 'That was Mr Gresham,' she said. 'He's decided to accept the Simpsons' offer after all.'

'So the age of miracles is still with us.' Simon grinned at her. 'I suspect that diplomatic pep talk you gave him about realistic property values, and the state of the market, may have swayed him a little.'

'And the fact that the Simpsons are offering cash may have had something to do with it too,' Alison reminded him drily. 'But I'm glad he phoned. Knowing the sale's going through makes me feel slightly less guilty about taking the rest of the day off.'

'Nonsense,' Simon said robustly. 'You deserve some time off. You've worked like a slave since you came back here—devotion above and beyond the call of duty.' He studied her with a slight frown. 'In fact I'm not sure it hasn't been too much for you. You're looking rather pale and wan these days.'

Alison bit her lip as she reached for her bag. 'I shall have to invest in some blusher,' she said lightly. 'Although having Melanie home for the school holidays will probably put some colour back in my cheeks.'

'She's a lively one all right,' Simon agreed. 'I haven't seen her for quite a while.'

'She should have been home on one of her weekend passes a fortnight ago, but she didn't make it,' said Alison with a slight shrug.

'Apparently there was something on at school.'

'And are you going straight to Mascombe Park to collect her now?'

'With a slight detour.' Alison paused. 'I'm having lunch with my mother-in-law first.'

'Poor you,' Simon laughed. 'No wonder you're pale!'

Alison smiled with an effort. 'No, it isn't at all like that,' she said. 'She's a darling. In fact, I wish I saw more of her than I do.'

Simon shot her a wry look. 'And does the same apply to her son?' He saw the rush of angry colour into her face and held up a placatory hand. 'I'm sorry—I'm venturing on forbidden territory, and I know it.'

'Then why say these things?'

'You know why,' he said heavily. 'I don't like seeing you neglected. You deserve better out of life than this, Alison.'

'How do any of us know what we deserve?' she said bitterly. She got to her feet. 'Well, I'll see you on Monday.'

Simon followed her through the reception area and out on to the pavement, standing, hands in pockets, watching while she reached in her bag for her car keys. The car, a sporty Alfa Romeo, had been delivered to Ladymead only a few days after Nick's departure to London, the usual curt memo from his office apprising her of its arrival. She'd tried to telephone, to thank him, but his secretary had told her he was in conference, and she had never been able to summon up sufficient courage to call again.

And as Nick hadn't paid even a fleeting visit to Ladymead in the three weeks since, that was how the situation remained between them.

She was grateful to Simon for giving her this job. It kept her days safely occupied, although it could do nothing to alleviate the misery of the lonely nights, tossing and turning in that enormous bed, her awakened, bewildered body crying out for surcease.

It was no wonder she was pale, although, with the passage of time, she had begun to suspect there might be a more cogent reason for her pallor than sleeplessness alone.

Simon said tentatively, 'You will be here on Monday? I didn't mean to pry, and I'd hate you to think you had to leave just because I can't keep my nose out of your private life.'

Alison straightened and looked at him. His probing had upset her, but she knew it was prompted by genuine concern, and her heart softened as she saw his boyishly abashed look.

'I know,' she said gently. 'And I shouldn't be touchy. You—you've been incredibly kind.' Impulsively she reached up and kissed him lightly on the cheek.

Before he could reach for her and hold her, she had stepped back and was getting into her car.

'Don't worry,' she called to him, as she drove off. 'I'll be back!'

It was a warm, sunny day, and she enjoyed the drive to Mrs Bristow's house, however much she might be dreading the inevitable tête-à-tête. But there was no way in which she could avoid it any longer. One more excuse and Mrs Bristow would be hurt, she realised. If her mother-in-law asked anything about Nick, she would just have to be very guarded. Yet Angela Bristow was no fool; she must have realised by now that there was something seriously amiss between her son and his new wife.

But there was nothing in the warmth of her welcome to suggest any reservations at all.

'It's so warm, I thought we'd lunch in the garden,' Mrs Bristow told her. 'Only a light meal—pâté, and a salade niçoise.'

'That sounds lovely,' said Alison.

'Hm.' Her mother-in-law looked her over shrewdly. 'I think perhaps I should have included something substantial, like a steamed pudding. You seem to have lost some weight.'

'Isn't that what everyone's trying to do?' Alison parried.

'If they need to—but you don't.' Mrs Bristow paused. 'Are you sure this job of yours isn't proving too much—with all your other responsibilities as well?'

Alison moved restively. 'I don't think so. After all, the house nearly runs itself these days.'

'And of course you have your mother to help you.'

'She does as much as she can,' Alison said neutrally, trying to dismiss from her mind the past weeks of carping and complaints from Mrs Mortimer. She had treated Alison's decision to go back to work as some kind of personal affront, and had become twice as demanding in consequence. And Nick's continued absence had inevitably become the target for a great deal of fretful and recriminatory comment.

'Can she drive?' asked Mrs Bristow.

Alison glanced at her in surprise. 'She certainly has a licence. My father insisted she kept it renewed, but I can never remember her behind the wheel of any of the cars we've had.'

'That seems rather a pity.' Mrs Bristow poured out sherry and handed Alison a glass. 'It would give her such a measure of independence. Has she started to go out at all?'

Alison sighed. 'Not really,' she admitted. 'She seems to prefer staying at home, although she does have visitors, of course.'

'Well, that's something.' Mrs Bristow leaned back in her chair and sipped at her sherry. 'But all in all, my dear, I can't believe your life is a very happy one.'

Alison felt that wave of betraying colour suffuse her face again. She said hastily, 'Oh, it has its moments. And Melanie comes back from school today. It always cheers Mother to have her around.'

'I can believe it,' Mrs Bristow laughed. 'I hope all the pressures of examinations won't stifle any of that sunny liveliness of hers. And that reminds me,' she added, 'she left one of her scarves here. I've been meaning to post it back to her at school, but you could deliver it in person, with my love, if you wouldn't mind.'

'Of course not,' Alison said mechanically, but her mind was whirling suddenly. 'I—I'd totally forgotten she'd been here.'

'Well, it was only a fleeting visit,' said Mrs Bristow. 'Nick brought her for tea on the way back to school. He probably didn't think it was worth mentioning.'

Alison noticed she had spilled a few drops of sherry on to her skirt. She rubbed at the marks with her handkerchief. Nick, she thought dazedly, taking Melanie back to school? But when? As far as she was aware, these past empty weeks he hadn't stirred from London. She'd thought his interests there were paramount, and all-encompassing, and now a casual remark had revealed that he had actually been in the district—

visiting her younger sister at school, taking her out. With a feeling of dread she recalled Melanie's rather confused and halting explanation why she couldn't come home a fortnight previously. Was that the reason—that she was spending the time with Nick instead?

Aloud, she said colourlessly, 'She's—very fond of Nick.'

'I'm sure it's mutual,' Mrs Bristow said serenely, unaware of the knife she was twisting in Alison's confusion of emotion. 'I was only sorry you couldn't be with them, dear, but Nick told me then how busy you were these days. Now, let's have some lunch, shall we?'

The food was tempting and delicious, but Alison had to force every mouthful past the tense muscles in her throat. But it was essential, she thought as she talked and laughed, to behave with complete normality. Angela Bristow must never know the shock her words had been.

It was a relief once lunch was over to be able to have a valid excuse to hurry away.

'It's been lovely to see you.' Mrs Bristow gave her a robust hug. 'And bring Melanie to see me during the holidays, won't you—I have great hopes of turning her into a gardener.'

Alison felt incapable of saying anything in reply to that, so she just nodded rather jerkily and got into the car, forcing a smile to her lips.

Once safely out of the village, she drew off the road on to the verge, and switched off the engine, leaning her forehead against her folded arms on the steering wheel.

Melanie, she thought incredulously, seeing Nick—and not saying a word about it. That was the important issue—the secrecy of it.

She bit her lip. Oh, she was imagining things. Melanie was just a child. Or was she seeing her merely as an older sister would, and disregarding the fact that Melly was a beautiful girl, rapidly ripening towards the maturity of womanhood? Lovely, vital and intelligent—and attracted to Nick. That was something she'd never made any secret of.

Surely Nick couldn't be such a bastard as to take advantage of the situation, she thought desperately. He was flattered, that was all. There couldn't be any more to it than that. He was a man of the world, after all, and Melanie was still only a schoolgirl.

Yet nothing could alter the fact that he'd deliberately sought her out, even while shunning Ladymead and its environs. Or had the approach come from Melly? She would probably never know.

One thing she had to face—if Melanie had been the older sister in her place, the marriage would have been conducted on very different terms. Melly wouldn't have allowed Nick to walk out after only one night, and return to his bachelor existence in London. But if Melanie had been the girl in his bed, perhaps he wouldn't have wanted to leave. She had all the attributes, after all, that any man would want in his wife.

And Melanie was plagued with none of her sister's uncertainties. She would know exactly what she wanted from life, and how to take it.

Had she decided, maybe, that she wanted her sister's husband?

Alison winced, pain lancing at her. It was no good telling herself that she was being a fool. Even fifteen years wasn't such an insuperable age gap, and Melly would be eighteen very soon, and in charge of her own destiny. Perhaps she thought her feelings for Nick were overwhelming enough to counterbalance the inevitable difficulties that any relationship with him would cause. Perhaps she even thought they outweighed hurting her own sister.

Or had Nick told her all the details of his hastily contracted, soon-regretted marriage, letting her believe that ending it would hurt no one? Apart from that one pitiful little confession of love, which he probably hadn't even heard, as she fell asleep in his arms, she had never given him any reason to believe she had any feelings for him at all, she realised sadly. Yet what else could she have done, when he had made it so clear to her that he wanted a marriage without any emotional ties? Perhaps meeting Melanie's fresh vitality had been what he needed to change his mind about that.

She wanted very badly to cry, to howl her wretchedness and rejection at the unfeeling sunshine outside, but that was impossible. Besides, she had no proof. There could be some entirely innocent explanation.

Oh God, she thought, as she started up the engine. There has to be.

The drive at Mascombe Park was choked with cars, as it always was at holiday times. Alison parked near the tennis courts and walked towards the main building, realising with a pang that this was the first time she'd fetched Melanie on her own. Always before, their father had been there too. The trips home had been hilarious, usually involving some lengthy detour and a lavish meal, or some other treat.

Today's homecoming would be subdued, for any number of reasons.

As she reached the front door she was pounced on by Miss Lesley, no less formidable because her face was wreathed in smiles.

'Ah, Mrs Bristow, how very nice to see you! May I take this opportunity of wishing you every possible happiness?'

'Thank you,' Alison murmured, as her hand was engulfed in Miss Lesley's firm hand.

'A sad time for you, of course,' the headmistress went on. 'But Melanie seems to have weathered the storm very well. Her work has hardly suffered at all. And of course, your husband has been a tower of strength. Such a charming man, and so generous. His donation to our building fund—the Sixth Form science block, you know—and then on top of that, last week, the gift to the library. We are so grateful to him.' She lowered her voice. 'And I'm sure his visits here have helped Melanie. The loss of a father can be terribly traumatic for a girl at her stage of adolescence. I don't normally allow the girls out of school except at the prescribed times, but I felt I could make an exception in this case. And your husband's visits have really perked her up.'

'I'm—glad to hear it,' Alison managed. Every word was like a death knell. 'We—we didn't want her weekends to be lonely.'

Miss Lesley laughed again, but her attention was passing, fixed on some approaching parents. 'Well, I can promise you they haven't been. And her classmates, I'm sure, have been most envious. Such a very attractive man,' she added with a kind of heavy roguishness. 'Ah, Mrs Henderson! How very good to see you again . . .'

Alison was released. She moved towards the stairs, her heart hammering slowly and heavily. It was clear Nick had been visiting Melanie every week—and the school would assume it would be with the approval of her family. He must have been very convincing to get past Miss Lesley, she thought unhappily. The headmistress might gush and tend to talk in clichés on this kind of occasion, but she was a shrewd woman and guarded her pupils with dragon-like strictness. A strictness which Melanie had often rebelled against, Alison recalled with a pang. Was that how it had all begun—through Melly's natural wish to shake off the shackles of boarding school life for a few hours?

She found Melanie throwing some last things into her case in the bedroom she shared with two other girls. She gave Alison a harassed look—or was it a guilty one? Alison told herself she mustn't read too much into things.

'I can't find half my stuff,' she declared tragically. 'I'm sure Jane and Helen just grab everything in sight when they're going home.' She dropped to her knees and began to root under the bed.

'What have you lost?' Alison asked.

'The scarf that Daddy brought me back from Paris.' Melly pushed her hair back from her face. 'I can't lose that—I just can't!'

It was in Alison's bag at that moment. All she had to do was produce it.

Instead she said slowly, 'Perhaps you left it somewhere.'

There was a pause, then Melanie said, 'I haven't been anywhere to leave it. It must be at home. Perhaps I didn't bring it back after half term.'

'That must be it,' Alison agreed, a hollow feeling in the pit of her stomach. 'Are these all your bags?'

'Yes, the trunk went to the station this morning.'

They were talking like strangers, Alison realised wretchedly, exchanging stilted platitudes. There was an awkwardness between them which she was not imagining, and a distance too. Melly's eyes had not met hers directly once since she had entered the room.

There was silence between them as they walked downstairs and out into the sunshine.

'How's Mummy?' Melanie asked at last.

'Much the same.' Alison kept her voice friendly and neutral.

'Well, that's hardly cause for congratulation!' Melanie's voice sounded sharp. 'Do you think it's a good thing for her to be living at Ladymead still? Mightn't a clean break have been better for her in the long run?'

'I don't know.' Alison concentrated on fitting the cases into the Alfa's boot.

'But surely you must give it some thought,' Melanie persisted. 'After all, it can't be good for her, sitting day after day, letting the rest of the world wait on her.'

Alison shut the boot. 'Is that a subtle way of telling me you're not prepared to run her errands?' She kept her tone pleasant.

'No,' Melanie returned defensively. 'But you must admit she expects a hell of a lot from us all. And you pander to her.'

'You've clearly been giving the matter a lot of thought,' Alison said crisply as she slid into the driving seat. 'Shall we wait until we get home before you start changing the world?'

'Well, there's no need to sound so fierce!' Melanie was clearly taken aback. 'I was thinking of you, that's all.'

'I'm grateful for the consideration,' Alison said ironically. 'And no doubt it had occurred to you that you'd have arranged things differently.'

'No question about it,' Melanie retorted. 'But then Mummy's never used me like she has you ...' She broke off abruptly. 'Look, we mustn't quarrel.'

'I hope we shan't,' Alison said quietly. 'Perhaps we should change the subject. What's been happening at school? Anything interesting?'

'At Mascombe Park?' Melanie asked derisively. 'It's a major event if a pigeon lands on the roof!'

'But there was something a couple of weeks ago.' Alison realised she was gripping the steering wheel far too tightly, and consciously made herself relax. 'When you didn't come home—a house drama competition, or something.'

There was a silence, then Melanie said, 'Oh— that. It was quite a giggle. Blue House won in the end.'

'It sounds fascinating.' Silently, Alison found she was praying, *Tell me that Nick came down and took you out. Make me feel ridiculous for even imagining such things, if that's what it takes. But don't let me go on like this—jealous and suspicious of my own sister!* Aloud, she said, 'I hope it was worth the sacrifice of a weekend at home.'

Glancing sideways, she saw Melanie's mouth curve in a small private smile. 'Oh, I think so,' Melanie said.

Nausea rose in Alison's throat, bitter as gall suddenly. She pulled over to the side of the road and thrust her door open, almost falling out on to the verge as she retched miserably on to the grass.

'Ally!' Melanie was kneeling beside her, ashen-faced, proffering a clean handkerchief. 'What is it? Are you ill?'

She straightened dizzily. 'No, of course not. I just felt rather—hot, that's all.'

'We'll open all the windows,' Melanie decreed briskly. She sent Alison a long look under her lashes. 'It is only the heat, is it? I mean—you're not planning to turn me into an auntie?'

The temptation to tell the truth—that her period was overdue, and she'd woken feeling slightly sick every day that week—was overwhelming. If Melanie knew there was a baby on the way, or even that it was a possibility, surely that might change any plans she and Nick might be making for the future. It could—or it could tie Nick to her through a sense of obligation. And that was the last thing she wanted.

She said shortly, 'Don't be ridiculous! Of course not. Now we'd better get going, before Mother starts imagining that we're upside down in a ditch somewhere!'

The first thing Alison saw as she turned into the drive was the car parked outside the house.

Melanie exclaimed joyously, 'Nick's here! That's fantastic!'

'Miraculous,' Alison said. It took a terrific effort of concentration to edge her car neatly alongside, but she managed it somehow.

Melanie flew into the house ahead of her, making for the study like some eager homing pigeon. Alison stood alone in the hall for a moment, staring ahead of her, then, moving slowly, she walked upstairs to her room.

She stripped off her dress with short, jerky movements, then went into the bathroom. She had a long cool wash, then cleaned her teeth, rinsing her mouth with meticulous thoroughness. Small things, but they made her feel a little better, physically if not mentally.

When she sent back into her bedroom, Nick was there, standing with his back to the window, his dark figure appearing grim and forbidding against the brightness outside.

Acting on reflex, she snatched up her discarded dress, holding it protectively against her.

His mouth curled in a smile that held no amusement whatever.

'Stop behaving like some threatened Victorian virgin,' he advised curtly. 'I came to ask if you were feeling better.'

Alison found a voice from somewhere. 'News travels fast.'

'Which would you prefer—my not knowing, or not being concerned?'

She shrugged. 'There's no need for concern,' she said dismissively. 'A slight tummy upset, that's all.'

'Are you sure?' He frowned critically, as his eyes went over her. 'You look like a ghost . . .'

'I'm fine. Now will you please go? I'm trying to get changed.'

'I'm not stopping you,' Nick said pleasantly. 'And I have seen you without your dress on before, if you recall—although I must say you looked considerably more seductive then than you do now.'

Alison flushed. 'It's not my intention to look seductive.' She felt foolish clutching the dress as if it was some kind of shield. She dropped it on to the bed and walked across to her wardrobe.

'Not for me certainly,' said Nick, an odd grimness in his voice.

Alison snatched a dress off the rail at random and pulled it over her head, twisting slightly as she tugged at the zip.

'Let me do it,' he said quietly.

She felt his fingers brush her skin, and her body convulsed in an anguish of yearning.

'Don't touch me!' she said stormily, pulling away.

Nick drew a sharp breath. 'Don't be a fool,' he said icily. She heard him walk away from her across the room, and then the door closing quietly behind him. Alison sank down on to the edge of the bed, and buried her face in her hands. She stayed like that for a long time. When at last she moved to the dressing table, she felt as if she was looking at a stranger. She was pale, as Nick had said, but even her bone structure seemed to have sharpened, the faint hollows beneath her cheekbones more pronounced than usual. She dragged a comb through her hair, and added a touch of colour to the strained lines of her mouth.

As she reluctantly approached the drawing room a few moments later, she could hear her mother's voice raised in some gentle complaint, and sighed.

As she walked into the room, she saw Mrs Mortimer seated in her usual chair beside the fireplace looking vaguely martyred, and Melanie standing at the window, her face flushed and mutinous.

'So far, my dear, tragedy has hardly touched you,' Mrs Mortimer was saying sadly. 'Youth is resilient, of course. But I would have expected my daughters—both my daughters—to have rather more understanding of the blow I suffered with your father's loss.'

It was a well-worn theme, and Alison took a firm hold on her patience.

'I'm sorry that we lack understanding, Mother,'' she said calmly. 'Would you like a sherry?'

'I certainly need some stimulant,' Mrs Mortimer acknowledged fretfully. 'It's rather hard, when one has scarcely seen one's younger child for weeks on end, to be taken to task as soon as she enters the house.'

'I was not taking you to task,' Melanie said crossly. 'I was simply enquiring if you'd been into the village at all since I was home last, or whether Ally was still running all your errands for you, as well as this house and her job.'

'I don't think I like your tone, dear,' Mrs Mortimer said reprovingly. 'I'm sure it's no bother to Alison to undertake the few little messages I have from time to time. Although heaven knows I hardly see anything of her these days,' she added with a sigh. 'I can't help but think she's over-committed her time by returning to Thwaites. After all, it isn't as if there's any financial need for her to work.'

'None at all,' Nicholas said pleasantly. None of them had heard him come in, and at the sound of his voice, Alison started, spilling a few drops of sherry from the decanter she was holding on to her dress. The blue eyes surveyed her sardonically for a moment before he went on, 'But clearly her job has other inducements apart from purely monetary ones.'

Alison replaced the decanter on the tray. 'Independence, for one thing,' she said coolly.

Her mother tutted. 'I suppose this is the modern viewpoint,' she said. 'But it seems to be a very extraordinary one for a married woman to adopt. When I married, I relied on my husband totally for my support.'

Alison handed her the glass, glad that her hand was steady. 'But these days,' she said, 'nothing is certain in this uncertain world. Marriages don't always last as long as they used to.'

'Alison!' Her mother's voice was sharp. 'What a thing to say! I'm so sorry, Nicholas. I don't know what ails either of my children today.'

Nick helped himself to a whisky and added a splash of soda. 'I can't speak for Melanie,' he said. 'But Alison tells me she's suffering from a bilious attack. Maybe it's curdled her outlook.'

'Well, it's the first I've heard of any bilious attack. I think she's doing far too much, undertaking a full-time job along with all her other responsibilities. I think you should put your foot down, Nicholas.'

'I intend to.' The merciless blue gaze seemed to take in every detail of Alison's pallor, the shadows beneath her eyes, before travelling down over the slender body beneath the clinging simplicity of her green dress. 'I've thought for some time that Alison does far too much.'

Alison set down her own glass with a thump. 'Perhaps you'd all be good enough to stop discussing me as if I wasn't here,' she snapped angrily.

'But then,' said Nick too pleasantly, 'you so rarely are here—darling.'

Alison's brows lifted defiantly. 'Is that really the problem?' she enquired. 'Or does it hurt your masculine pride to have a wife who works? I don't feel I neglect any of my commitments.'

Nick's glance was openly derisive, as he swallowed the remainder of his whisky. 'Perhaps that's something we should discuss later—in private,' he said. 'Now, shall we go in to dinner?'

It was not a comfortable meal. Mrs Mortimer kept up a flow of bright, inconsequential chat which only served to underline the taciturnity afflicting the rest of the party, rather than conceal it.

Melanie was the quietest, Alison recognised with a pang. Head bent over her plate, her sister was picking desultorily at her food. Perhaps the problems of conducting a love affair with another woman's husband under their own roof were just beginning to come home to her, she thought unhappily. Perhaps she was undergoing the same agony of jealousy that Alison herself was lashed by.

God, what a mess! she thought as she pushed her plate away.

When the meal was over, she stood up. 'I think I'll have an early night,' she said. 'See if I can throw off this virus.'

'That's an excellent idea,' Nick said softly. 'Go and get some rest, darling. I'll be up very soon.'

His smile challenged her. Words of defiance rose in her throat, and were choked back. But he'd banked on that, she thought stormily, as she walked towards the door. He knew she wouldn't make a scene in front of her mother—and Melanie, of course, whom he must have hurt by this hypocritical display of husbandly concern.

As she went upstairs, she heard the dining room door open, and quickened her step, panicked by the thought that Nick might be following her already. Her heel caught on the edge of the stair, nearly dragging her shoe off completely in the process. She paused in mid-flight, bending to retrieve the errant footwear, and heard from the hall below Melanie's voice, low and urgent, saying,

'Nick, I must speak to you. It's all going wrong. What are we going to do?'

She heard their footsteps going down the hall, then the soft closing of the study door behind them.

Alison found she was gripping the banister rails so tightly that the polished wood was bruising her hands. She sank down on to the step and sat there staring numbly down into the shadowy hall beneath. She heard, as if from a distance, the warning stir of the grandfather clock as its sonorous Westminster chimes prepared to proclaim the hour. It was one of the familiar reassuring sounds of her life, part of the home that had always been hers—the home she had fought to save. The home she had sold herself to save.

But the security she had paid so highly for no longer seemed to exist.

Crouched there on the stairs, Alison had never been so lonely or so afraid in her life.

CHAPTER NINE

SHE would have run, but there was nowhere to run to. Yet how could she bear to stay here and suffer this humiliation? Images of Nick and Melanie together—holding each other—touching and kissing—kept presenting themselves to her tortured mind. They were willing, it seemed, to run any risk of discovery rather than deny their feelings for each other, and the thought made her shiver.

Well, she wouldn't stand in their way. She couldn't. And at least she could comfort herself that Nick had no idea how stupidly and hopelessly his unwanted wife had fallen in love with him. That was a secret she would carry within her until the day she died.

She put a hand lightly and protectively on her abdomen. This was one secret she would be unable to conceal for very long, and its existence would bring a whole train of new problems in its wake. She had no idea how Nick would react to the reality of being a father. When he had asked her to marry him, he had made it clear it didn't enter into his plans at all. Perhaps it was an attitude he would maintain. Besides, if it was Melanie he wanted, would he really want to be saddled with any reminders of his brief first marriage?

'I'd have to go away,' Alison thought. It would be less embarrassing for everyone, and it would save her the pain of having to see Nick with Melanie, and know that he no longer belonged to her.

Not that he ever had, she thought sadly, but for a while she had been able to pretend.

She had taken refuge on the window seat in her bedroom, but now she was beginning to get cramped and even a little chilly. With a slight start, she realised she had been sitting there for over an hour. She got down stiffly, shaking the creases out of her dress, then paused, immobile, her attention totally arrested as the door opened and Nick walked into the room.

'Don't look so startled,' he advised cynically as he closed the door behind him. 'You can't pretend you weren't expecting a visit from me.'

She found a voice from somewhere. 'And I thought I'd made it clear that I didn't want to be disturbed.'

'Perhaps I chose to consult my own wishes instead,' he said. 'I have to talk to you, Alison, and this seems to be the only place where I can be guaranteed not to have some kind of audience.'

'I don't want to talk,' she protested. 'I—I'm not feeling well.'

The dark brows lifted. 'Then your upset clearly isn't the temporary thing you tried to make out. I'd better get you a doctor.'

'No!' She was aware of the panicky note in her voice, and made a grab for composure. 'I don't need a doctor. Just some rest.'

'Then why aren't you in bed already?' he demanded. 'Stop twitching like a cat on hot bricks. I'll say what I have to say, and then get out, if that's what you want.'

'That is precisely what I want.' She lifted her chin and met his gaze full on.

'That sounds remarkably like a gauntlet being thrown down,' Nick remarked softly. 'I'm tempted to test your stony resolve, my sweet.'

Alison took a step backwards. 'Leave me alone,' she said bleakly. 'This confrontation was your idea, not mine.'

'That's certainly true,' he agreed. 'I get the impression that no power on earth could make you voluntarily agree to be alone with me.'

She shrugged. 'Why should I make a secret of it? And why should it matter to you anyway? I'm sure you don't go short of—alternative company.'

His eyes narrowed. 'I don't think there's anything to be gained by pursuing that particular line,' he said coolly. 'Although it fits in with what I've come to say to you, in a way.' He paused. 'I think it's obvious to us both that things can't continue as they are. I think the time has come to put an end to this travesty of a marriage, and . . .'

'And you want a divorce?' Alison interrupted. Speaking the actual words herself might make them easier to bear. 'Yes—I agree. And as soon as possible.'

There was a long, almost stunned silence. Eventually Nick said, 'Just like that?'

'Did you think you were such a great matrimonial prize that I'd hang on to you at all costs?' Alison queried, investing her tone with icy sarcasm. 'No, I'm as keen to regain my freedom as you are. I think a clean break is best. I—I shan't make any demands on you. I'm working, and I get a reasonable salary. I don't want alimony.'

'You're not being offered it,' he said curtly. 'And I think the whole matter requires a little more discussion, although I can understand why your freedom, as you put it, should suddenly seem to attractive to you. Perhaps while you still bear my name, you and your lover could restrain your public demonstrations of affection.'

She stared at him. 'What the hell do you mean?'

'I like the injured tone,' he said cynically. 'I'm sorry I didn't warn you I was arriving today, so that you could be a little more discreet. As it was, I was an interested eye-witness as you and Thwaite took your fond farewell of each other in full view of the entire market square.'

'I don't know what you think you saw,' Alison began, but he interrupted, his voice savage.

'I don't think, darling, I know. I saw you kiss him, and I had plenty of time to observe the way he was looking at you. He's clearly besotted with you.'

'You're totally mistaken,' she protested. 'That— that was just a friendly gesture.'

'Oh, stop all this injured innocence,' Nick snapped with cutting impatience. 'I suppose I should have expected it. You did warn me, after all, my darling, that you weren't prepared to live like a nun. And we both know, don't we, how deeply those still waters of yours run. It's a pity you couldn't have found yourself a more exciting lover.' He walked forward, and again Alison was forced to retreat. He said, 'Perhaps we should compare notes, although my experience of you may well be more limited than his. Does he know, for instance, that when you reach your climax, your eyes change from cool hazel to bright green, like a little cat's?'

Blood burned its way into Alison's face. She lifted her hands and pressed them to her ears. 'Don't,' she begged. 'You're wrong—quite wrong. And—even if . . .' She hesitated.

'Yes?' he prompted chillingly. 'What were you going to say?'

Her teeth sank into her lower lip for an instant. 'That—you have no cause to reproach me. Or are you trying to pretend that you've been a model husband since our marriage?'

'I don't know what a model husband is,' he said coolly. 'It sounds very dull.'

'And that sounds very evasive.' Her voice shook a little. 'But there's no need to play with words, Nick. You see—I know.' She swallowed. 'I know that you've been seeing Melanie secretly.' As his face darkened, she went on hastily, 'Oh, I don't blame her. She's very young and impressionable, and you must seem very glamorous to her. I always knew she tended to have a—a crush on you. And in all ways, she'd make you a more suitable wife. I—I don't pretend otherwise.'

There was a silence. Then, 'That's very gracious of you,' he drawled. 'You've really got it all worked out, haven't you? Melanie for me, and Thwaite for yourself. How civilised! We could make up a four at bridge.'

She winced. 'Don't! Isn't it better to try to be— civilised about these things?'

Nick shrugged. 'That depends on your viewpoint, I suspect. Besides, civilisation is only a veneer, my sweet. Threaten any one of us, and you'll find pure caveman underneath. Or has no one ever warned you about that?' He took another step forward.

The edge of the bed was pressing against the backs of her legs and she couldn't retreat any further.

'Please don't do this.' She was ashamed to hear how tremulous her voice sounded. 'I suppose your pride is hurt because I want out of this marriage as much as you do.'

'Now that I doubt,' he said harshly. 'And I think my pride will survive, even if a little dented. God forbid that I should keep you tied to me and miserable.'

There was a note in his voice that seared along her nerve-endings.

She said, 'This way, neither of us need be miserable again.' She couldn't meet his gaze. 'And now that we've said—all we need to say—perhaps you'd go, and leave me in peace.'

'Peace?' Nick asked savagely. 'What's that? I don't think I've known a moment of it since I laid eyes on you. You'll have years of—peace ahead of you, if that's what you want, once we've been through the divorce court. But in the meantime, we're still married to each other, and I intend to take full advantage of the fact!'

His arms went round her, dragging her against him, then she was crushed—suffocated under the burning pressure of his mouth.

She tried to struggle, to push him away, but he was too powerful, too determined, lifting her off her feet to put her down on the bed, following her down while that endless, draining kiss still went on.

She could hardly breathe. She certainly couldn't speak or resist, and suddenly she knew she didn't want to. If this was to be their farewell to each other, then, however it had begun, she would cherish every moment of it.

When at last Nick took his mouth from hers, she didn't speak. Instead, she lifted her hands and stroked his hair, following the growth of its springing thickness down to the nape of his neck, her fingers sliding round to caress the strong column of his throat.

He drew a deep, unsteady breath and began to touch her in turn, his hands rediscovering the slender curves of her flesh, the delicate planes and angles of her body's bone structure through the thin material of her dress.

He handled her, she thought dazedly, as if she was some rare and precious object, all too easily broken. Yet she was broken already—control, pride, self-respect all smashed to tiny pieces on the wheel of her yearning for him.

Already in these few brief moments she was faint with wanting him, her head light, her body, heavy and languid, welcoming the hardening, urgent pressure of his against her. It was a need she recognised and shared.

Nick sat up, lifting her with him, holding her for a long time breast to breast while his lips touched her face in a myriad tiny kisses, falling like honeyed fire on her responsive mouth. At last he turned her gently in his arms, and she felt his fingers part the smooth fall of her hair, and his lips touch the back of her bared neck. She shivered as his mouth traced a path down between her shoulder blades to the neckline of her dress. He took the metal tongue of her zip between his teeth and tugged it down, his hands stroking the dress from her shoulders, letting the fabric fall in a soft pool around her hips. He unhooked her bra and slipped the fragile straps down her arms, so that there was no further impediment to the passage of his mouth down the long delicate curve of her spine.

Alison arched her back in instinctive, sensual delight, and gasped as his hands slid round her to cup the urgent thrust of her breasts, his fingers a warm torment on the sensitive peaks. She made a little sound in her throat as her whole body convulsed in wanton physical craving.

She twisted round to face him, kneeling on the bed, pushing away the crumpled dress with shaking hands, watching him, her eyes fever-bright.

Nick shrugged off his jacket and tossed it to the floor, unknotting his tie with swift taut movements. She waited while he took the thin gold links from his cuffs, but when he began to unbutton his shirt, she stopped him. She was trembling violently, and it made her clumsy, tugging impatiently at the fabric as she freed the buttons, but at last it was done, and she could touch him as she wanted to, stroking the palms of her hands across the width of his shoulders and down over his chest, watching the flare in his eyes as her fingertips stroked and caressed. She leaned forward and kissed him, sliding the tip of her tongue along his lower lip, brushing his nipples deliberately with her own.

He took her by the hips, his hands sliding inside her lace briefs to find the silken flesh beneath, moulding and exploring until he reached the warm, moist eagerness of her, and lingered. She moaned, moving restlessly against his hand, urging him to pleasure her.

Reality had totally receded. There was nothing in the world but this room, this bed, this man, his weight pressing her down into the softness of the mattress, his mouth exploring the naked vulnerability of throat and shoulders and breasts, his whole being tautly concentrated on the warm, sensual frenzy his caresses were arousing in her.

She wanted so much more—tried to tell him so in a voice she barely recognised as her own. Nick lifted himself away slightly, freeing himself from the remainder of his clothes, and then he was with her as she had yearned for him to be, her body melting and supple as she received him, his strength and warmth encompassed in her grace.

Their mouths met and clung heatedly, mirroring the passionate exchange of their bodies. Alison discovered reserves of desire in herself, depths of response she had never suspected she was capable of. She clung to Nick, arms and legs twined fiercely round him, her hands stroking the sweat-dampened skin of his back as he urged her with him beyond all the limits of experience, beyond any wildest dream.

The release, when it came, was anguished, almost frightening in its intensity. She was crying out soundlessly, her body splintering in an intensity of pleasure, holding him closer and closer as she tried to absorb the moment and make it last for ever.

She thought deliriously, He's mine. And then, ice closing round her heart, she remembered . . .

And with remembrance came a bitter shame that she had allowed this to happen—wanted so desperately for it to happen.

Nick's arms were wrapped round her, his mouth tracing small lazy patterns on her breasts, his body still joined with hers. A little sob rising in her throat, Alison tried to disengage herself.

He lifted his head slightly and smiled at her, the blue eyes filled with an expression that almost stopped her heart.

'Wait,' he told her softly, his voice a promise.

Her hands came up and pushed at his bare shoulders.

'I'd like you to go, please.'

Nick looked at her again, but this time there

was no warmth or tender beguilement in his expression.

He said quietly, 'I beg your pardon. Would you mind repeating that?'

'I want you to go,' she said. 'I want you to leave me alone. You—you had what you wanted and . . .'

His hand closed round her chin, not altogether gently. 'You little hypocrite! It was entirely mutual and you know it.'

'You don't need to remind me. I'm already deeply ashamed.'

'Are you, by God?' The sudden harshness in his voice grated across her nerve endings, making her wince. 'But there's no need to be, my prudish wife. Sex, after all, is like any other appetite. Once it's been stimulated, it needs feeding. You're in no way abnormal.'

Her whole being cringed. To hear the joy they had shared reduced to that level was almost more than she could bear. If he'd struck her, the shock could not have been deeper.

She said, 'Thank you for the reassurance, but that isn't exactly what I meant.'

'I'm all for clarity,' Nick said softly. 'And at any other time I'd be delighted to hear what your tortuous little mind has decided to use as an excuse this time. But not now. At the moment I have other things in mind—and allowing myself to be turned out of your bed isn't one of them. You mustn't be so niggardly with that charming little body, my sweet. I've paid a tall price for the privilege of keeping you in the manner to which you're accustomed. Surely you can steel yourself to—accommodate me once in a while?'

Alison said in a tiny, thin voice, 'You have no sense of shame at all, do you?'

'Not where you're concerned, darling. On the contrary, I feel like a man who's discovered treasure in his own backyard.'

'With Melanie as an additional bonus?' she asked bitterly. 'Do you never suffer from scruples?'

'Never.' Insolently, he bent and brushed her mouth with his. 'Either professionally or personally. Isn't that what you expected me to say?'

'I suppose so,' she said wearily. 'I always knew you had your own idea of morality. Why should a minor point like an arranged marriage change anything?' She paused. 'But don't think for one moment that Melanie would take any act of infidelity as lightly.'

'Oh, I wouldn't.' The blue eyes glittered down at her. 'I knew from the first that you were very different propositions. At the moment, of course, she eats out of my hand. But I don't expect this idyllic situation to continue for very long.'

Her voice cracked slight. 'You—you will be kind to her?'

'Naturally,' he said. 'As a matter of fact, it's very easy to be kind to Melly. She's—extremely receptive. After you, sweet wife, it's something of a relief to be with a woman who thinks I'm wonderful, and isn't fighting me tooth and nail every step of the way. And now, let's change the subject.' The practised hand slid the length of her body in sensuous command. 'I may as well make the most of what little time with you I have left.'

Hot tears scalded her eyes suddenly. 'You're vile! Doesn't it matter to you that she'll probably guess where you are, and be hurt?'

'She knows exactly where I am,' Nick said coolly. 'She was very understanding.' He bent to one rose-tipped breast, tugging the tumescent peak gently with his lips.

The burning pleasure of his hands and mouth on her skin was already having its inevitable effect, carrying her away on a swift and painful tide of feeling she was unable to resist.

While she was still able to speak, she began, 'You can't . . .'

'Oh, but I can,' he said softly. 'And I will. I intend to have something to remember from this—travesty, darling, before you push me out of your life for ever.'

'Damn you,' she muttered hoarsely, her body arching involuntarily to meet the first, powerful thrust of his. 'Damn you . . .'

And was engulfed in a storm of sensation which threatened to tear her apart. This time there was no finesse in their coming together, and no reticence either in the harsh, sobbing silence as they took endlessly from each other, Alison's own demands as fierce and overwhelming as those of the man who drove her remorselessly to the end of endurance itself.

When it was over, she lay spent and shaken beneath him, the tears raining helplessly down her face. As, at last, Nick lifted himself away from her, she had to dig her nails into the palms of her hands to prevent herself from reaching for him, clinging to him. She'd promised to free him; she couldn't renege on that. Nor did she want his pity.

She pressed her clenched fist against her teeth, biting at the knuckles, damming back the words that must never be uttered. If she spoke, she would plead, and she couldn't do that; what little self-respect she still possessed forbade it.

She was aware of the shift in weight as Nick left

the bed, and heard the soft sounds of movement as he retrieved his clothes and began to dress.

At last there was a silence deeper than she had ever known.

His voice broke it bleakly. 'You can have your divorce,' he said. And the door closed behind him in utter finality.

CHAPTER TEN

It seemed impossible that she should ever sleep, but eventually she did—and awoke to Mrs Horner bringing in her tea, just as if it was any other day.

'The weather's nice,' Mrs Horner announced, pulling back the curtains. 'They reckon it's set fair for the weekend. Pity Mr Nick couldn't stay down here and relax for once instead of chasing off back to London.'

Alison pulled herself up against her pillows. 'Has he gone already?' She tried to make it sound the most normal thing in the world.

'At the crack of dawn, according to Cook.' Mrs Horner directed a look of mild censure at Alison. 'You should get him to relax more, Miss Alison, or he'll be making himself ill.' She headed for the door. 'Oh, and your mother's asking for you,' she volunteered. 'Seems in a bit of a state.'

Alison groaned inwardly. 'I'll go to her as soon as I'm dressed.'

She felt dead inside, but life was dragging her relentlessly back into the familiar groove, and she supposed she would be grateful for that, as she showered and dressed hastily in jeans and a loose top.

Mrs Mortimer was sitting in her usual chair by the window when Alison entered, bright spots of outrage burning in her face.

'Just what is the meaning of this?' she demanded, thrusting a sheet of paper at Alison.

Alison's brows drew together. The heading

across the letter indicated that it came from one of the local driving schools, and, addressed to her mother, it informed her politely that the driver's refresher course which had been booked in her name would commence that afternoon at two o'clock, and that her instructor Mr Robert Hargreaves would call at the house.

Alison read it through and shrugged. 'I don't know,' she said. 'Perhaps it's a mistake. Maybe there's another Mrs Mortimer in the locality.'

'If there is, then I've never heard of her,' her mother dismissed the idea with an angry wave of her hand. 'They're touting for custom, obviously, and you must telephone them at once, and tell them their tactics are a disgrace. I have no intention of driving again—there's no need. You're perfectly capable of taking me anywhere I want to go.'

Alison said mildly, 'If you could drive, it would give you added independence, Mother. After all, I may not always be here.'

Mrs Mortimer's bosom swelled. 'And where else would you be, I'd like to know? Are you implying that the occasional lift—the odd favour, is too much trouble for you?'

It occurred to Alison that she would not describe the unceasing daily demands on her time and patience in quite those terms, but she knew from bitter experience that even to hint as much would lead to one of those painful, tearful scenes from which her mother invariably emerged in triumph, so she said merely, 'Of course not. I was just thinking of you. You could pop over and see Aunt Beth whenever you wanted, for one thing. And Mrs Bristow has asked several times for you to visit her.'

Mrs Mortimer wore her stubborn look. 'It's far simpler for them to come here,' she said. 'My health is rarely good enough to tempt me to undertake any kind of journey. You must make that clear to people, Alison. They seem to forget what I've had to suffer this year. They can be so thoughtless sometimes. Even Melanie annoyed me very much yesterday evening—almost interrogating me, if you please, about where I'd been, and what I'd been doing.' She gave an angry little laugh. 'Rather like the Spanish Inquisition! She's a child, of course, and can't be expected to understand my feelings, and so I told her.'

'I don't think Melly intended to be—insensitive,' Alison said slowly. 'I'm sure she has your well-being at heart.'

'Then she should realise I want to be left in peace with my dear memories.' Mrs Mortimer gave a little sigh. 'And this house is so full of them still, in spite of all the changes that your husband has seen fit to make,' she added with a touch of acidity. 'He seems extremely restless, Alison. Mrs Horner tells me he's left us again. He said nothing about it at dinner last night.'

'I think some problem blew up.' Alison wondered bleakly how her mother would react to the news that her marriage was over. As long as her own comfortable existence wasn't threatened, she would probably not be particularly concerned, she decided.

Her mother tutted. 'I must admit I find the atmosphere more peaceful when Nicholas is away. He tends to have a disruptive personality.' She leaned back in her chair and closed her eyes. 'Now, please go and tell this driving school that its services will not be required.'

Melanie was hovering in the hall as Alison came downstairs.

'Has the post come?' she asked.

'Yes.' Alison gave her a steady look. 'Were you expecting a letter?'

'Not exactly,' Melanie admitted, her eyes fixed on the paper in Alison's hand.

'I see.' Alison flicked the corner of the paper. 'Do you know something about this, perhaps?'

'Mummy's driving lessons?' Melanie nodded. 'Of course I know. Don't you think it's a marvellous idea?'

'In theory, it's all right,' Alison said drily. 'In practice it's impossible. I'm ringing up to cancel them.'

'Oh, but you can't!' Melanie protested at once. 'I mean, they won't. Nick arranged it that way. He said she'd want to get out of it if she could, and that the school weren't to accept any excuse, but turn up as arranged.'

Alison's brows snapped together in shock. 'Nick—said that?'

'Well, of course.' Melanie gave her an appealing look. 'You mustn't be angry with him. Mother is the limit, you know, expecting you to wait on her hand, foot and elbow all the time. And it's not good for her to stay upstairs in that room, thinking martyred things. You know it isn't.'

'I'm not arguing,' Alison assured her. 'I know it's not healthy, but I haven't found any successful method of budging her, or even getting her to face ordinary life again.' She paused. 'And even if the driving school car arrives, as you say, I don't know how we can persuade her out of her room and into it.'

'Oh, Nick will manage that,' said Melanie with

supreme confidence. 'She's a wee bit in awe of him, you know, and if he puts the pressure on, she'll do as she's told.'

Knives turned slowly in Alison's heart. 'I see,' she managed, and walked into the dining room. She touched the coffee pot, aware her hands were shaking, and hoping that Melanie, who had followed her, hadn't noticed. 'I think I'd better ring for some fresh.'

'Where is Nick anyway?' asked Melanie.

'Not here.' Alison pushed the sugar basin to the other side of the milk jug as if her life depended on it.

'Oh,' Melanie said blankly after a pause. 'You mean he's gone out—or is he still in bed?'

'Don't you know?' Alison gave her a straight look. 'Didn't he tell you he was going back to London?'

'What?' The sound was a yelp, Melanie's face a picture of consternation. 'Oh, no, I don't believe it! And without a word to me. Oh God, what am I going to do now?'

In spite of the pain she was feeling, Alison experienced a pang of sympathy for her sister. Melanie was so young, so vulnerable to be passionately involved with someone like Nick. He was in love with her now, but would it last?

She said quietly, 'It—seemed better if he went. But I'm sure he'll be in touch with you.'

'In touch?' Melanie echoed incredulously. 'What the hell is the use of that? I need him here.' She paused, then said awkwardly, 'There's something he wants to talk to you about—something you may not like, but—oh, Ally, I'm sure it's for the best in the long run. Things can't go on as they are, and you look so pale and tired. I know you're not happy.'

'No.' Alison summoned up a smile from somewhere. 'No, I haven't been happy, but you won't make my mistakes.'

'Well, I don't think I'd have taken the whole thing on in the first place,' Melanie said. 'Although at the time, I must say it was a relief. But we should have known it wouldn't work.'

'No.' Alison swallowed. 'Mel, I'd rather not talk about this now. I—I've spoken to Nick, of course, and told him that I know what's been—happening, and that I won't make waves, and I promise you the same thing—only I'd prefer not to discuss it any further now.'

Melanie grimaced. 'I'm afraid you're going to have to,' she said, glancing rather distractedly at her watch. 'And if you've talked everything over with Nick, I'm amazed he didn't tell you about the driving lessons. Oh, damn Nick! Why the hell did he have to go haring off back to London, and leave us to face the music? Mother's bound to make a scene when she finds out, but she wouldn't have dared if Nick had been here.'

'I won't let her,' promised Alison. 'I won't let her be angry with you—either of you.'

'Hm.' Melanie pulled another face. 'Don't think you'll get away unscathed either. She'll probably tell you that you've betrayed her—that we all have. But honestly, Ally, I know we're doing the right thing.'

'Please.' Alison was shocked at the sudden violence in her voice. 'I've told you—I can't talk about it now. Do you think I have no feelings at all?'

Melanie suddenly looked very young and very vulnerable. 'That's the last thing I'd ever have thought,' she said in a small voice. 'I know what Ladymead means to you.'

'Ladymead?' Alison laughed harshly. 'Do you think that's all I care about? My God, there are times I wish the place had burned to the ground!'

Melanie's face cleared a little. 'Well, that's what I told Nick. I said I was sure when it came down to it you'd feel like that. But Nick wasn't certain and . . .'

'Nick—Nick—Nick!' Alison's voice cracked. 'Do you have to keep saying his name? I've asked you not to discuss this now . . .'

'Ally!' Melanie had gone white. 'What's the matter? What's wrong with you? I thought you were in agreement?' She broke off abruptly, as the front door bell sounded imperatively. 'Oh, hell, that'll be Mrs Lambert here already. I'll answer it—unless you want to?'

'Mrs Lambert?' Alison said wearily. 'Who on earth is Mrs Lambert?'

'Nick didn't tell you about her either?' Melanie stopped, and put a repentant hand over her mouth. 'Look, I'd better let her in,' she went on as the bell sounded again.

Alison followed her out into the hall. The woman waiting on the doorstep was tall with a calm, humorous face. As she took in Melanie's obvious tension, and Alison's white strained face, her brows lifted questioningly.

'Good morning,' she said. 'I'm Freda Lambert, and I understood I was expected, but it seems I may have arrived at a bad time.'

'Expected?' Alison asked rather dazedly. 'I don't quite understand.'

'You'll be Mrs Bristow, of course.' Alison found her hand taken in a warm clasp. 'Your husband told me he would explain everything to you before I came, but perhaps his courage failed him. He wasn't sure how you would react to the idea of your mother having a paid companion. Maybe he thought it would be better to present you with a *fait accompli.*'

'Perhaps he did.' Alison felt stunned, but rallied. 'Won't you come into the drawing room, Mrs— er—Lambert, and I'll arrange for some coffee.'

'Perhaps hot sweet tea might be better,' Mrs Lambert said with a twinkle. 'Isn't that the sovereign remedy for shocks? I'm sorry my appearance has proved so traumatic for you. I'm sure Mr Bristow intended you to find it a pleasant surprise. Isn't he here? He said he would be.'

'I'm sorry,' Alison said awkwardly. 'He—he's been called away on business.'

'What a shame,' Mrs Lambert sympathised. 'When the whole point of my being here is to allow the two of you more freedom, and more time together.' She paused. 'Would it be better, do you think, if I met your mother before we have coffee?' She gave Alison a dry smile. 'That might give her time to get over her initial annoyance and resistance to the idea first.'

'I think that's a marvellous plan,' Melanie put in hurriedly. 'I'll take you up to her.' To her sister she muttered, 'Sit down, Ally, before you fall down. You look as if you're going to faint!'

'I feel as if I am,' Alison said helplessly. 'I'd like to know exactly what's going on, please?'

'It's quite simple.' Mrs Lambert's tone was soothing. 'Your husband has engaged me, Mrs Bristow, on a month's trial as a companion for your mother. He feels that since she was widowed, she doesn't quite realise how many demands she makes on your time and energy, and that you, as her daughter, find it impossible to tell her so. So—

my first task is to get her to accept me, purely on a temporary basis, then we'll go on from there.'

'She never will,' said Alison, giving her a straight look.

'Oh,' Mrs Lambert's twinkle deepened, 'stranger things have happened. Of course, if you don't want us to make the attempt—if you feel it would be better if I left now, without seeing her, then, quite naturally, I'll go along with that. But I wish you'd let me try.'

Alison sank down on the sofa. 'Very well,' she said at last.

She sat alone, staring into space, trying to make sense of what was happening and failing, until Melanie returned, and she was able to round on her. 'Do you mind telling me what's going on? Or are you simply—clearing the decks, because you're not prepared to look after Mother, as I've done?'

Melanie stared at her. 'What difference can it possibly make to me?' she asked, as if she was reasoning with a lunatic. 'I'm not here ninety per cent of the time, anyway. No, the problem is yours—and Nick's, of course. But I thought you'd had all this out with him?'

'No.' Alison moistened dry lips with the tip of her tongue. 'I—misunderstood you. We—were discussing something rather different. Surely you must realise that?'

Melanie shrugged. 'If you say so. But it seems odd when I know Nick intended to get the whole thing straight with you this weekend.' She paused, as if a thought had struck her. 'Ally, when Nick told you what he wanted, what he's going to do— you didn't quarrel, did you?'

Alison's hands were clenched tightly in her lap. 'You—could say that,' she admitted tonelessly.

'So that's why he's gone off like this!' Melanie looked horrified. 'Ally, you shouldn't have been angry with him. He's only thinking of you, after all. And himself, of course,' she added as a cautious amendment. 'After all, it can't be much fun for him having Mother living in the same house, always there whenever he comes down here, and always making her presence felt—because she does, Ally, and if you're honest, you can't deny it. She likes to be the centre of attention, and it's only natural for Nick to want you to himself, especially when you've only been married for about five minutes. And she will like Mrs Lambert, when she gets used to the idea—I know she will. It was the house that Nick was concerned about. It meant so much to you, he said, held so many memories that you might not want to give up. But he feels stifled here. You can't blame him for wanting to find somewhere with no past associations for either of you. And Mummy needs to be independent too. That's really what Mrs Lambert is for—to coax her back into the real world again, as Nick says.'

Alison lifted her hands to her head. 'I don't understand any of this. There's nothing to stop Nick leaving. I—I never thought he'd stay here—with you.'

'With me?' Melanie asked in a peculiar tone. 'Where do I come into all this?'

'Don't let's play any more games,' Alison begged unhappily. 'I know you've been—seeing Nick. I don't blame you, Mel, honestly. I always knew you had a thing about him from the very first, and in all sorts of ways, you're far more suited.' She swallowed. 'But, darling, you're so young. Are you sure you know your own mind—that you aren't just infatuated?'

It was Melanie's turn to sit down abruptly. The faint sprinkling of freckles across her face stood out against her sudden pallor.

'You know?' she said slowly. 'And you thought that I—that Nick . . .? Oh, Ally, how could you have been such a fool! Yes, I've been seeing him. He's been so desperately unhappy, and he needed someone to talk to—someone to consult about what he could do to put things right between you. Eventually he brought his mother in on it too, and we hammered out a plan between us. The driving lessons were part of it, and Mrs Lambert, of course. And—and selling Ladymead. A whole new start for you both. He was going to talk to you this weekend, try and persuade you to agree.' She paused. 'Surely you didn't tell him what you suspected?'

Alison's lips felt numb. 'Yes.'

'Strewth!' Melanie was silent for a few minutes. 'And when he told you the truth, you argued with him?'

'He didn't deny anything,' Alison said in a low voice. 'I—I said I wanted a divorce, and he—he agreed to give me one.'

Melanie looked as if she was going to burst into tears. 'Oh God, that's awful! It must have killed him. Yes, of course I adore him—who wouldn't? But apart from the fact that he belongs to you, he's too old for me.' She gave a wobbly smile. 'And if I had been in love with him, I'd have got terribly fed up, because all he ever wanted to talk about was you. He's crazy about you. Surely you know that?'

'No,' Alison said steadily, 'I didn't know. I've got everything hopelessly wrong, and somehow I'm going to have to put it right. If I can. If it's not too late.' She paused. 'Can you cope here—you and Mrs Lambert?'

'Of course,' Melanie said instantly. 'But what are you going to do?'

Alison got to her feet. 'I'm going to find him.'

As she went to the door, a desperate, soundless prayer welled up inside her, 'Dear God, please don't let it be too late . . .'

She was close to panic when the taxi dropped her at the door of the elegant mews house. She stood there, staring at the pristine gleam of fresh paintwork and brass, wondering what welcome, if any, awaited her. Wondering, too, if she should have phoned in advance to warn Nick that she was on her way. To find out, if she was honest, whether there was any point in her journey, or whether all that awaited them in the future was the bitter finality of separation and divorce.

Leaving Ladymead had not been easy. Her mother's protests had been voluble and tearful.

'But you never go to London!' Grievance rang from her voice and stared from her eyes. 'You hate the place. Alison—I've heard you say it a dozen times.'

'But Nick is there,' Alison said gently. 'I'm going to be with my husband.'

Mrs Mortimer sniffed pettishly. 'I fail to see why Nicholas can't come here instead. He seems very restless—and extremely keen to cause as much uproar in other people's lives as he can,' she added angrily. 'I shall find it very hard to forgive him for this day's work. Foisting some—stranger on to me in this extraordinary way! Well, she can go. I want nothing to do with her. And I shall have a number of things to say to your husband if he ever deigns to show his face here again!'

'You must do as you please, of course,' Alison said levelly. 'But perhaps it might be better not to part with Mrs Lambert too quickly. I don't know when I shall be coming back, and you'll need someone to run your errands for you, and keep you company. And she seems extremely competent and pleasant.'

'She's also a keen walker, and a member of some Advanced Motorists association.' Mrs Mortimer sat very upright, two bright spots of colour burning in her face. 'I will not be manipulated in this way! How can you allow it, Alison?'

Alison's smile was small and twisted. 'I have my own life to put in order,' she said.

Melanie was waiting in the corridor when she emerged. 'Go,' she ordered briefly. 'I'll look after Mother, and get her into a better frame of mind. She can't sit in that room feeling sorry for herself for the rest of her life. She's still a comparatively young woman.' She put her arms round her sister and hugged her fiercely. 'Be happy. I've packed a case for you.'

'But you don't know what I need—what I want to take,' Alison protested half-heartedly.

Melanie gave her a catlike smile. 'I've made an educated guess,' she said. 'Now, be off with you.'

It was only a small case, but it seemed as heavy as lead as Alison carried it across the narrow road, and rapped at the door.

It was answered almost at once by a middle-aged woman wearing a neat overall over a dark dress. Her smile was polite, but her eyes narrowed when she saw the suitcase at Alison's side.

'May I help you, madam?'

Alison moistened her lips. 'This is—Mr Bristow's house?'

'It is.' The woman's tone remained civil, but forbidding. 'Are you expected? Mr Bristow mentioned nothing about visitors.'

Alison lifted her chin. 'I'm Mrs Bristow,' she said quietly.

'Well, I never!' the other exclaimed helplessly. Her smile broadened. 'Come in, Mrs Bristow. I hadn't the least idea you were arriving. Mr Bristow never uttered a word—and he's out too.'

'It was an impulse.' Alison stepped into a narrow, thickly carpeted hall. 'I hope it's not inconvenient,' she offered awkwardly.

'Never in this world. If I've asked Mr Bristow once, I must have asked him twenty times when he was going to bring you here, but he's always said you prefer country life. This is a real pleasure, I must say.' The woman lifted Alison's case and carried it down the passage. 'I'm Doris Gordon,' she added over her shoulder. 'I've worked for Mr Bristow ever since he first came to live here. It's a pretty house, but small. Not big enough for a family,' she added, giving Alison a shrewd, top-to-toe assessment that brought the colour flooding into her face.

'Oh, dear.' Alison bit her lip. 'Is it that obvious?'

'Only if you know what to look for,' Mrs Gordon assured her kindly. 'And you look just like my eldest girl did, madam. Been a bit sick too, I daresay, but that'll soon pass. Now, this is the main bedroom,' she added, throwing open the door.

It was a comfortable room, but the décor and furnishings were uncompromisingly, even starkly masculine. It was hardly the kind of love nest where Alison had imagined Nick entertaining his ladies.

'Shall I unpack for you, madam?' The question brought her sharply out of her reverie.

'Er—no,' she said quickly, remembering Melanie's feline smile. 'I'll do it.'

'Then I'll make you some tea,' Mrs Gordon said briskly. 'It'll be ready in the drawing room as soon as you are.'

Her instinct had been quite right, Alison discovered as she opened the case. A wry smile tugged at the corners of her mouth, as she lifted out the sinuous lingerie that Aunt Beth had given her, and the red dress she had bought for that first dinner party, and never worn. All her prettiest and most seductive clothes, in fact.

The drawing room was upstairs, a big room overlooking the walled patio garden to the rear. As well as tea, Mrs Gordon had provided thin cucumber sandwiches and a featherlight Victoria sponge.

'You need feeding up,' she said with a martial light in her eye as she set the tray down. 'There's no excuse for looking washed out when you live in the country.'

In spite of her inner turmoil, Alison drank two cups of tea, and demolished all the sandwiches, and two slices of sponge, winning an approving smile from the housekeeper when she returned.

'Mr Bristow did say he wouldn't want me this evening,' she said rather doubtfully. 'But I'll be happy to stay if you want me to.'

'Oh, no,' Alison assured her. 'I'm sure you have your own plans. I'll be quite all right.'

'Well, if you're sure.' Mrs Gordon was clearly relieved. 'I usually leave about now, unless Mr Bristow's giving a dinner party, of course. Although there aren't as many of them as there were when he was a single gentleman.'

Alison bent her head, 'I suppose not,' she acknowledged quietly.

She'd been under a number of misapprehensions, it seemed. And this house was one of them. It was pretty, as Mrs Gordon had said, but it had a curiously unlived-in atmosphere. Apart from the books, shelved in the alcoves that flanked the elegant fireplace, and the collection of records racked beneath the hi-fi unit, there were few signs of Nick's occupancy. It was a place—somewhere to come back too, but no more a home for him than Ladymead had been, she realised suddenly. And realised too how lonely he must have been.

She had gone into this marriage thinking only of her own security and stability, and that of her family. She had never considered Nick's needs at all. He was wealthy and powerful, therefore he had to be self-sufficient too. She had kept house at Ladymead, but she had never attempted to make a home for him, to create a refuge against the pressures of his working life.

She had been hurt because he came to Ladymead so seldom, she thought ruefully. Now it seemed incredible that he had ever been there at all.

It seemed odd too to look through the books and find many of her own favourites among them. She knew so little about his tastes, after all. That brief cool courtship had been totally unlike the usual voyage of exploration that two people make at the beginning of a relationship.

She wandered restlessly round the house, wishing he would come home, but dreading the moment at the same time. In the neat kitchen, she found steaks and the makings of a salad in the refrigerator. She decided to prepare a *gratin dauphinois* to go with them, and that gave her an occupation for a while.

But the time afterwards dragged endlessly. Mrs Gordon clearly had no idea where Nick was, she thought. Supposing he did not return at all? Perhaps he had already written off his short, disastrous marriage, and had sought out one of his past loves.

She was slumped bonelessly in an armchair listening to Delius's 'Brigg Fair' on the hi-fi, and staring into space, when at last she heard the rattle of a key in the lock.

She sat up, her fingers digging sharply into the padded arms of the chair. It seemed a very long time before she heard Nick's step on the stair.

Then the drawing room door opened, and he walked in.

He looked tired, she noticed immediately, and strained, his mouth set in the lines of cynicism she detested.

He said, 'I already have a housekeeper here.'

'I've met her,' Alison told him. 'I—I haven't come to—usurp her position.'

'Then may I know what you have come for?'

He wasn't making it easy for her, she thought, but then why should he? Aloud, she said, 'I—I've come to be with you.'

'How nice,' he said harshly. 'You don't want me as a husband, but I'll fill the bill as a tame stud. Is that it?'

'No!' Her voice lifted in a kind of anguish. 'No, you don't understand. Please—please let me explain.'

He shrugged. 'What is there to explain?'

Alison said in a low voice, 'The way I've misjudged you, first of all. I've been stupid and very blind. I'm sorry.'

His mouth twisted. 'Really? I've always known what a bloody low opinion you had of me, but I must admit I never expected to be accused of seducing a child like Melanie.'

Alison bent her head. 'I know,' she said wretchedly. 'But I found out you'd been seeing each other without a word to me—and she does care for you, Nick—more than she'll admit, I think.'

He nodded expressionlessly. 'She has a slight crush,' he said. 'Nothing I can't handle, and nothing that will survive the first glimmer of a man of her own on the horizon. I thought, knowing her, you'd have had the wit to appreciate that for yourself.'

She swallowed. 'I wasn't thinking very clearly.' She looked at him appealingly. 'And—you—you didn't deny it.'

'Why should I?' he demanded roughly. 'From where I was standing, it seemed as if you were grasping at straws—that you wanted to be rid of me at any price. How the hell could you have believed, even for a moment, that I thought of Melly as anything more than your kid sister?'

'I suppose I was too jealous to make much sense of anything,' she said quietly.

'Jealous?' Nick smiled bitterly. 'I don't think you even know the meaning of the word. I thought, like a fool, that I could make you care for me. That first time in bed together, I thought I'd actually succeeded. You told me you loved me before you fell asleep, and I felt as if I'd been given the world. I lay awake for hours making all kinds of plans to carry you off with me and spoil you to death in every way there was, but the next morning we were suddenly as far apart as ever.'

He sighed. 'You made it more than clear that it was your house and your family which mattered to you. I was there on sufferance, and that was all.'

'Oh, but you're so wrong!' Alison beat her hands together in distress. 'I—I'd known for ages I was in love with you, even on our honeymoon, but I was scared to let you see—in case you rejected me.' Her face burned. 'I'd seen newspaper pictures of some of the women you'd been involved with in the past, and I knew I couldn't compete.'

There was sheer incredulity on Nick's face. He said gently, 'But you never had to compete, my darling. All I was praying for was one look from you, one sign.'

'But you said all those things,' Alison pointed out almost inaudibly. 'You said you didn't want any commitment—that you didn't believe in love, even.'

Nick groaned. 'I said altogether too much,' he said ruefully. 'In my own defence, I have to say I was in a pretty confused state. I'd known, you see, when your father first approached me for that money, that it could all go wrong, and I tried to warn him—to deter him, but he wouldn't listen. But that didn't stop me feeling guilty about it. And the fact that you obviously despised me caught me on the raw too. Yet, at the same time, I was intrigued. It was such a contrast to the kind of dull politeness you'd treated me to when I sat next to you at dinner.'

Alison gasped. 'You weren't exactly charming yourself!'

'I had other things on my mind,' he said frankly. 'I was there to finalise the deal with your father, and I was damned uneasy about it.' He paused. 'I asked you to marry me on an impulse I barely understood myself, although I think now it was the beginnings of love, even though I didn't recognise it as such.'

'When did you?' She had to know.

'That day in my mother's garden,' he said slowly. 'There you were beside me, and it seemed so utterly right that you should be. I knew without question that what I wanted from life was you at my side for ever. But I was scared stiff because I knew I'd ruined everything with all that talk of contracts and bargains. I couldn't suddenly blurt out that I loved you, because you'd never have believed me, and I might have lost you. So I decided to bide my time.' He paused. 'The honeymoon was hell. I felt all the time as if I was treading on eggshells. You seemed to bristle every time I came near you, except for that last night.'

'I remember.' Alison smiled a little.

'So do I,' he said. 'For the first time since I'd met you, you felt totally warm and yielding in my arms. I had to force myself to go off to my stateroom alone, but when I got there, I couldn't rest.' He looked at her. 'It may sound crazy, but I seemed to hear you calling to me—wanting me, so I came to you, hoping, only to have my eyes nearly scratched out for my trouble.'

She said in a muffled voice, 'You weren't mistaken, I was calling to you. But then I got scared too. I thought you just wanted to use me— because I was there, and you needed a woman.'

Nick said softly, 'No, love. It was you, and only you. I was crazy for you. That's why I stayed away from Ladymead so much. I thought not seeing you might make the ache easier to bear, but it didn't. I began to wonder if you were really as happy with your precious bargain as you insisted, and it occurred to me that what really stood between us was that damned barracks of a house, and your mother's never-ending demands. So—I talked the whole thing over with Melly, and came to the conclusion that the only chance I had of winning you was to free you from all of it.' The blue eyes met hers squarely. 'I want to sell Ladymead, Alison. Taking it on originally seemed the answer to a number of problems, but it's simply created others instead. And your mother is neither elderly nor feeble, just reluctant to take responsibility for her own life. I think it would be good for her to have a place of her own. But what I need to know is, does the house—the past—mean so much to you that you want to hang on to it at any price?'

Alison shook her head, slowly and determinedly. 'I want you, Nick,' she said. 'Nothing matters to me but you. I'll go wherever you want.'

There was a long silence, as they looked at each other. He said, 'I love you, Alison. Marry me. Be my wife.'

He held out his arms and she went into them like a homing bird, her heart soaring in joy as he held her.

She said, 'For ever, Nick,' and he repeated the words like a vow.

After a while, he said huskily, 'Isn't it time we began our honeymoon?'

She hid a smile in the front of his shirt, pressing closer to him as she did so. 'But I've got food ready. Don't you want dinner?'

'Later,' he said, and lifted her into his arms to carry her to the bedroom.

A long time afterwards, when the first sweet storm of passion had spent itself, they lay, quietly relaxed, in each other's arms, saying all the things they had never said, asking the questions neither of them had ever dared frame before.

'And you're handing in your notice to Thwaite,' Nick said suddenly, lifting himself up on one elbow. 'Or I won't be responsible for my actions!'

She smiled teasingly. 'Poor Simon! How can I leave him in the lurch?'

'Quite easily.' Nick kissed the tip of her nose. 'That'll teach him to keep his hands off other men's wives!'

'So you were jealous too,' she marvelled. 'There was no cause.'

Nick's mouth twisted in wry tenderness. 'Being in love doesn't always make one exactly rational,' he admitted. 'As you've also found out, my darling. Besides, I've discovered an alarming tendency in myself to be jealous of everyone and everything with even the slightest claim to your attention. I'm not proud of it, and I will try to overcome it.'

'You'd better,' she smiled, thinking of the one sweet secret she still had to share with him.

With a sigh of sheer contentment, he pillowed his head on her breasts, his lips paying tribute to their scented fullness. 'Just as long as you know that it won't all be moonlight and roses,' he said sleepily.

'All the best roses have thorns,' Alison whispered.

And whatever problems there would be, she thought, seemed a very small price to pay for the happiness of being Nick's wife at last.

Harlequin Presents

Coming Next Month

Available in November wherever paperback books are sold, or through Harlequin Reader Service:

In the U.S.
P.O. Box 1397
Buffalo, N.Y.
14240-1397

In Canada
P.O. Box 2800, Postal Station A
5170 Yonge Street
Willowdale, Ontario M2N 6J3

ATTRACTIVE, SPACE SAVING BOOK RACK

Display your most prized novels on this handsome and sturdy book rack. The hand-rubbed walnut finish will blend into your library decor with quiet elegance, providing a practical organizer for your favorite hard-or soft-covered books.

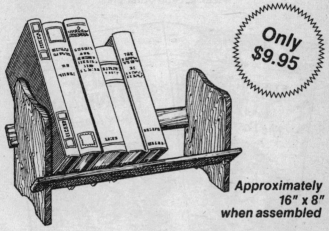

Only $9.95

Approximately 16" x 8" when assembled

Assembles in seconds!

To order, rush your name, address and zip code, along with a check or money order for $10.70 ($9.95 plus 75¢ postage and handling) (New York residents add appropriate sales tax), payable to *Harlequin Reader Service* to:

In the U.S.

Harlequin Reader Service
Book Rack Offer
901 Fuhrmann Blvd.
P.O. Box 1325
Buffalo, NY 14269-1325

Offer not available in Canada.

BKR-1